D0857002

THE
CHATTERING
CHIMP CAPER

THE CHATTERING CHIMP CAPER

•

(Book Twelve)
in
The Jennifer Gray Veterinarian Mystery Series

•

GEORGETTE LIVINGSTON

AVALON BOOKS
THOMAS BOUREGY AND COMPANY, INC.
401 LAFAYETTE STREET
NEW YORK, NEW YORK 10003

PRINTED IN THE UNITED STATES OF AMERICA
ON ACID-FREE PAPER
BY HADDON CRAFTSMEN, BLOOMSBURG, PENNSYLVANIA

For my husband, Bill. This one is for you,
my love, for putting up with so much. . . .

Chapter One

Wondering what could be more wonderful than spending a lazy Saturday afternoon in the town square, listening to the Calico High School band play a medley of romantic, easy-listening tunes, Jennifer Gray leaned back in her lawn chair. She smiled at her handsome, white-haired grandfather, who was obviously enjoying the music as much as she was. "Glad you decided to come with us, instead of spending the afternoon hammering?"

Emma Morrison spoke up. "Well, if he's not, I am. Your granddaddy has been work-

1

ing entirely too hard remodeling that old bell tower, and it's time he took a little breather.''

Wes frowned at Emma. ''And you know what they say. Don't put off until tomorrow what you can do today. I'm glad I came, you understand, but now I'll have twice as much to do on Monday. Before you know it, it will be fall, then winter, and . . .''

Emma let out a harrumph. ''If you'd taken my advice and hired a professional crew of carpenters, the whole project would be finished by now.''

Wes waved a hand. ''I'm the pastor, and that's my church, Emma, and the Wilson boys are doing just fine. For sure, it's kept them out of trouble.''

Emma pursed her lips. ''Well, summer isn't over yet, Wesley Gray, and in case you haven't noticed, those two are showing all the signs of boredom, and spend more time drinking lemonade than hammering nails. Why, just yesterday, I caught one of 'em snoozing under a tree. I shook him awake, and told him to get back to work, or I'd call his mama.''

Wes grunted. "No wonder he kept looking over his shoulder all afternoon. Poor kid probably thought you were going to tie him to a fence post and give him twenty lashes."

Emma had been the Grays' housekeeper for years, but she was also a wonderful part of their family, loving and caring in every way. She also enjoyed a good verbal sparring match with Wes, who seemed to delight in goading her on, too. Jennifer had learned at a very young age it wasn't serious; it was simply their way, making them even more lovable and dear.

Normally, Jennifer wouldn't take sides, because it was a losing proposition, but this time she had to agree with Emma. Her grandfather had been working too hard, and she was grateful he'd agreed to take this little respite.

The sparring match forgotten, Emma gave Jennifer a satisfied nod. "It's good to see you relaxing, too, young lady. Though I suppose your smile would be a little brighter if Ken would stop taking all those pictures and join us." She looked at her

4 *Georgette Livingston*

watch. "It's almost two, and I told him we were going to eat at two."

The amphitheater facing the stage where the band was playing was filled to capacity. But as usual, they had decided to sit on one of the grassy knolls, under a sprawling shade tree. They'd brought along a blanket and lawn chairs, and a picnic basket filled to the brim with delectable treats. But they hadn't opened it yet, because they wanted to wait until Ken Hering could join them. At the moment, he was still mingling with the crowd, taking pictures for the morning edition of *The Calico Review,* though he was slowly making his way toward them.

"He'll be here at two," Jennifer returned, "because he adores your fried chicken."

Emma's blue eyes flickered over Jennifer's yellow sundress, and her mouth dimpled in a grin. "My fried chicken isn't the only thing he adores. You look mighty pretty today, young lady. Don't you think so, Wes? Wes?" Emma rolled her eyes. "Well, if that isn't the ticket. Will you look at him! He's gone to sleep on us. Now, if

that doesn't prove he's overly tired, I don't
know what does.''

Wes opened one eye. ''I'm not asleep,
Emma. I'm just trying to concentrate on the
music.''

The band was playing ''Moon River''
now, one of Jennifer's favorite songs, and
she sang along, trying to remember all the
lyrics. But before she'd reached the end of
the first stanza, her pager beeped.

''Uh-oh,'' Wes said, opening both eyes.
''It must be an emergency at the clinic.''

Jennifer pulled the pager from her tote,
saw it was the phone number at the clinic,
and sighed. ''Ben wouldn't be paging me
unless it was a major emergency. Sorry.
Tell Ken I'll call him later, and save me
some chicken?''

Wes nodded. ''We'll save you a little bit
of everything, sweetheart. Drive carefully?''

Jennifer said she would, gave kisses
around, and hurried toward her Jeep
Cherokee.

* * *

The Front Street Veterinary Clinic was a few miles west of town, and it was an easy drive. Jennifer made it in just a few minutes, and although she was prepared to handle any emergency, nothing could have prepared her for the sight of the Cromwell sisters' ragtag truck parked in front of the clinic. The sisters only had one pet, a wonderful little chimpanzee named Peaches, and just the thought of her being ill or injured sent Jennifer on the run.

She found Ben Copeland, her partner in the clinic, with the sisters and Peaches in the emergency examining room, and quickly gave Peaches a visual assessment. She didn't appear to be injured or ill, just highly agitated, and upon seeing Jennifer, she raised her long arms and screeched.

"Thank heavens you're here!" Frances Cromwell exclaimed, shoving her granny glasses up on her nose. "I told Fanny that little Jennifer Gray would know what to do. We've been nearly sick with worry."

Fanny bobbed her head. "Worried and scared. She's been actin' goofy for the last few days, but it got worse today. Ben took her temperature and said it's normal, but . . .''

Ben waved a hand. ''Let's let Jennifer examine Peaches, and go from there, ladies.''

Peaches had her long arms around Jennifer's neck in a death grip, and there was no way she was going to let go. ''Come on, sweetie,'' Jennifer said gently. ''You'll have to let go if I'm going to examine you.''

Peaches responded by shrieking again, and burying her face against Jennifer's chest.

Jennifer sighed. ''Okay, let's try a different approach. Let's go sit in the little garden behind the clinic, and just pretend everything is normal. Maybe that will help calm her down. As I recall, she loves orange soda. Do we have any left, Ben?''

Ben nodded. ''Coming right up.''

''Sittin' in the garden ain't gonna do it,'' Fanny muttered. ''We tried that at home this mornin', and she ended up tramplin' the petunias.''

"Well, we have to give it a try again," Jennifer said, heading for the back door.

The sisters followed, plodding along in their calf-high boots, and although they'd been reluctant, they both smiled when they saw the garden.

"This is nice," Frances said, sitting down in a wrought-iron chair. "Who planted all the flowers?"

"Ben's wife, Irene," Jennifer said, taking the chair under the large elm tree. "She thought we needed a place where we could take our breaks, and get away from the clinic's medicinal smells."

Fanny sat down beside the small table, and sighed. "It's a real pretty spot, but I still don't think it's gonna help Peaches none. Look at her, a-hidin' her head."

Frances and Fanny Cromwell were large, rawboned women with wild gray hair, startling blue eyes, and leathery skin. Called "the crazy Cromwell sisters" by almost everybody in town, because they made moonshine in a bathtub and wore long black dresses and boots, they also had hearts as big as the moon. And Peaches meant everything to them. Today they had Peaches dressed in pink rompers, and Jennifer could smell baby powder. In their eyes, she was their baby, and their concerns were normal and justifiable.

A few minutes later, Ben brought out a can of orange soda and a squiggly straw. He was a tall, rugged-looking man with an easy smile, but at the moment, his smile looked forced. ''Peaches didn't want me to touch her, Jennifer, and I found that a little odd, because she's usually so friendly.'' He popped the top on a can and handed it to Jennifer, along with the straw. ''This one hasn't been in the fridge long, so it shouldn't be too cold.''

''Come on, sweetie,'' Jennifer coaxed. ''It's orange soda, and Ben even brought you a squiggly straw.''

Peaches looked at the can and pulled her lips back from her teeth in a typical chimp smile, only now, it looked more like a grimace. But she finally took a few sips.

''That a girl,'' Jennifer cooed. She looked at the sisters. ''You say she's been acting 'goofy' the last couple of days?''

"That's right," Frances said. "Might even be longer than that, now that I think about it."

"Has anything out of the ordinary happened this past week?"

Frances nodded. "We bought a new truck."

Fanny said, "It ain't new, but it runs better than the old one. I know, you saw our old truck out front. That's 'cause Frances don't like drivin' the new one 'cause it's an aut-tee-matic."

Jennifer shook her head. "I don't think buying a new truck would cause a behavioral problem."

"We bought new dresses," Frances said. "Pretty flowered ones, and we bought new boots."

"Don't forget, we bought them blue coveralls, too, sister," Fanny announced. "Oh, and we put new curtains up in Peaches's bedroom. Pretty pink ones with lots of lace. Matches her bedspread."

Jennifer smiled. "The fact that you've actually gotten Peaches to sleep in a bed is quite remarkable, but so far, I can't see where any of it—the truck, your new clothes, or the pink curtains—would cause this kind of problem. Has she been eating?''

Fanny bobbed her head. "I wanted to give her some of our elixir, 'cause it cures everything from ingrown toenails to warts, but I remembered what you said when we got Peaches from those nice circus folks. Her little digestive system wouldn't take to it, so we've been real careful.''

"We changed the brand of diapers we were using," Frances said thoughtfully. "Bought a couple of boxes of those really pretty ones with little flowers.''

Ben said, "That doesn't sound like something that would put her in a snit. Have you had any visitors? Somebody who might have teased her or been mean to her when you weren't looking?''

Frances glared at her sister. "Go on, sister. Tell them all about Zacharias Hardy.''

Fanny squared her shoulders and looked down her nose at her sister. "Zacharias Hardy would never do anything to hurt Peaches. But while we're on the subject, suppose you tell 'em all about Charlie Biggs, sister.''

Jennifer said, ''Doesn't Zacharias Hardy owns the farm across the road from you?''

''That's right,'' Frances replied. ''And Fanny is sweet on him. Every time I turn around, he's at the house trying to help her with her chores. Before we lost the old homestead to the bank, Zacharias's wife was still alive. She was a nice lady, and I thought he was a nice man.''

''Zacharias *is* a nice man,'' Fanny snapped. She looked at Jennifer and shook her head. ''His wife died 'bout three years ago, during that time we was livin' out in that little cottage on Marshton Road. When we got the money to buy the old homestead back from the bank, nobody was happier than Zacharias. That's 'cause he was lonely.''

''Lonely my foot!'' Frances exclaimed. ''He's a gold digger. The only reason he's so happy we're back in the old house is because he knows we came into all that money. Wasn't no secret, sister. There was even a story about us in *The Calico Review*.''

Fanny stomped a booted foot. ''Well, at least Zacharias owns his farm, and don't have to muck out barns for a livin'.''

Frances lifted her chin. ''Charlie Biggs doesn't muck out barns. He's in charge of the milking machines.''

Fanny made an upward spiral motion with her index finger, as if to say, ''Big deal.''

''So who is Charlie Biggs?'' Ben asked.

Frances smiled. ''Why, he's just the nicest man. He works for Elmer Dodd at the dairy.''

Fanny scowled. ''And seeing's we live right next door to the dairy, that man is always comin' over to eat his lunch. Or Frances is always goin' over there, carrying a picnic basket on her arm. Can't imagine why she'd want to eat close to all those smelly cows. Bad enough to be a-livin' right next door, and get that smell when the wind is up. I missed our house all those years we was gone, but I surely didn't miss those cows.''

Frances clucked her tongue. "Charlie is a widower, too, and he's lonely, sister."

"And he's probably seein' dollar signs every time he looks at you."

"Charlie doesn't know one thing about the money," Frances insisted. "He wasn't even living in Calico when all that happened."

Fanny snorted. "And you think he hasn't heard the talk? Are you forgettin' old Elmer Dodd had to pay us for land his daddy took illegally? Are you forgettin' Elmer is Charlie's boss?"

Frances wagged a finger under Fanny's nose. "No, I'm not forgetting, but Charlie Biggs isn't the type to listen to gossip."

Fanny rolled her eyes. "You're blind, sister. Blind as a bat and about as stupid!"

At that moment, Peaches let out a wail, and tried to scramble away from Jennifer. And just as quickly, Jennifer had the answer. "Have you two been squabbling at home?"

Fanny muttered, "Fightin' would be more like it. And we're gonna keep right on fightin' until I knock some sense into Frances's head.''

''Even at the expense of Peaches's happiness? Don't you see? It's probably your fighting that has caused her emotional upheaval.''

''We bicker all the time,'' Frances said flatly. ''Never a day goes by in our life that we don't bicker, and it's never bothered her before.''

Jennifer sighed. ''But this is more than bickering, Frances. And what's even more amazing, you're fighting over a couple of men.''

Ben said, ''Is it possible Peaches is jealous?''

''I'm more inclined to believe she's upset because of all the fighting,'' Jennifer said, ''but I suppose it's possible. How does she behave when the men are around?''

''She won't have anything to do with either one of them,'' Frances admitted. ''As a rule, she stays in her room.''

Jennifer nodded. ''She probably associates the two men with your fighting. We've known all along, contrary to what her original owners thought, that Peaches is a very intelligent animal, and it goes without saying she loves the two of you very much.''

Fanny's eyes filled with tears. ''And we love her, too. She's our whole life.''

Ben cleared his throat. ''Well, not quite, ladies. You've added a couple of men into the equation.''

Jennifer went on, ''Worse, you are battling over them. If you don't mind, I'd like to make a suggestion. If you insist on fighting, do it when Peaches isn't close by, and let's see what happens.''

''Then you ain't gonna examine her?'' Fanny asked.

''I'll examine her as a precaution, but she looks pretty healthy to me. You've taken wonderful care of her physically, but now I think you'd better concentrate on her mental happiness, as well as your own.'' Jennifer stood up. ''Come on, Peaches, let's take a look at you, so the sisters can take you home.''

Peaches kept her arms wrapped firmly around Jennifer's neck, but this time when she pulled her lips back over her teeth, it was a genuine smile.

Jennifer winked at Ben, and headed into the clinic.

"Charlie Biggs?" Emma said, lifting a brow. "I've never heard of him."

Wes shook his head. "I haven't heard of him, either. You say he's working at the dairy?"

Jennifer had gotten back to the town square in time to hear the band play the last song, and now, after telling everybody what had happened, she was busily eating fried chicken, baked beans, and Emma's wonderful coleslaw while they discussed the puzzling dilemma.

Ken Hering ran a hand through his red hair, something he always did when he was thinking, and then he smiled. "I'll bet Charlie Biggs is that tall, rugged, white-haired man I met in John, Jr.'s, office the other day."

"What was he doing in John, Jr.'s, office?" Jennifer asked.

"He brought in some advertisement

copy for Elmer. Elmer is going to have a special on eggs next week, and didn't want to run it with his usual ad.''

Emma muttered, ''John Wexler, Jr., co-owns *The Calico Review* with his daddy, and he is also the managing editor. I say he should put a stop to Elmer's shenanigans. Elmer buys eggs from all the local farmers for a song, and then doubles, even triples, the price for the consumers. I say if Elmer is going to sell eggs, let him raise his own chickens!''

Jennifer licked her fingers, and grinned. ''Speaking of chickens, you've outdone yourself this time, Emma. The fried chicken is fantastic.''

Ken stretched out on the blanket, and put his hands behind his head. ''Well, I sure pigged out. So, the sisters are fighting over their boyfriends. It's hard to picture them with one man in their lives, let alone two.''

''Do you think Peaches is jealous?'' Wes asked thoughtfully.

''That's what Ben said, and I'm not counting it out, but I think all the fighting is the real issue. They've promised to keep it down to a low roar, so we'll see what happens.''

Emma pursed her lips. ''Can't imagine any man being interested in those two.''

''Now, now,'' Wes scolded. ''You're supposed to be looking on the inside, and you know those two have beautiful hearts.''

Emma snorted. ''Pickled hearts, you mean, what with all the moonshine they drink. Zacharias Hardy. That old coot. It wouldn't surprise me one bit to find out he's after Fanny's money. He fell on hard times after his wife died, and almost lost the farm.''

''But he didn't,'' Wes reasoned. ''And now his crop of corn is just about as good as anybody's around. I think he had to have time to mourn after Edith's death, that's all, and now he's ready to get on with his life. And so what if that includes a lady friend or two?''

Jennifer said, ''The sisters bought new flowered dresses. Wonder if Zacharias and Charlie were the motivation?''

Wes chuckled. ''Well, anything would

be an improvement over those long black dresses. Poor little Peaches. She was getting all the sisters' attention, and now she has to share.''

Emma clucked her tongue. ''And that's what love is all about, Wes. Sharing.''

Wes's blue eyes twinkled. ''Then you're willing to share the rest of your lemonade? There isn't one drop left in the thermos.''

''There isn't one speck of cake left, either,'' Emma said, ''and we promised to save a little bit of everything for Jennifer.''

''I can do without the calories,'' Jennifer said, waving her hand dismissively at the picnic basket.

Ken stretched lazily. ''Then I guess I couldn't talk you into walking over to Fenten's Ice Cream Parlor for a cone? Triple scoop, and I'll buy.''

Wes reached into his pocket, and pulled out a ten-dollar bill. ''I'll buy if you'll bring us home a quart of chocolate fudge ripple.''

Emma frowned. ''We have a perfectly good ice-cream maker at home, Wes. If you want ice cream, just say so.''

"Ah, but can you make chocolate fudge ripple?"

Emma's pretty mouth turned down. "I prefer strawberry ripple."

Wes handed the ten-dollar bill to Ken. "Should be enough there for a quart of strawberry ripple, too. And don't forget to get a bag of candy sprinkles."

Chapter Two

Jennifer received the frantic call from Frances Cromwell the following morning while she was getting ready for church, and wasted no time getting out to the sisters' house on East Dairy Road. Peaches was having a screaming fit again, and this time she was up on the roof and wouldn't come down.

It had taken Jennifer nearly an hour to coax Peaches to shinny down the birch tree near the house, and now Jennifer was sitting in the sisters' wonderful country kitchen, drinking tea and trying to get to

23

the bottom of the latest tantrum, though it seemed more like an anxiety attack to Jennifer. Frances had put Peaches in her room, and for the moment, she was quiet.

"I know you think we were fighting again," Frances said glumly, "but we weren't. We got up early to do our chores, and we weren't even together when that hullabaloo started."

Both women were wearing blue coveralls, and Fanny hitched the straps. "That's right. We wasn't even together. Can't stand Frances's bad mood in the mornin', so I usually do the outside chores, and she does the inside. Along 'bout eight, when she can keep a civil tongue in her mouth, we get together for breakfast."

Jennifer looked at the wood-framed clock on the wall. "It's after ten. Have you had breakfast?"

"Ain't hungry," Fanny muttered.

Frances clucked her tongue. "Well, I'll bet little Jennifer Gray is hungry. Bet we pulled her away before she had a chance to eat one bite."

"It doesn't matter," Jennifer said. "All

I was going to have was a piece of toast, and one of Emma's banana smoothies.''

Frances made a face. ''What on earth is that?''

''She puts bananas and skim milk in the blender, and you drink it like a milk shake.''

Fanny said, ''Sounds like something Peaches would like, though she'd probably like it made with peaches better.'' Fanny looked up at the ceiling. ''It's awful quiet up there. Maybe I'd better look in on her.''

''I'll go,'' Jennifer said, ''and then we'll try to reconstruct everything that's happened from the time you left the clinic yesterday.''

The sisters had done some wonderful things to the old house after buying it back from the bank, and although Jennifer visited them often, it was always a delight to see the polished floors and dark wood furniture, and the bowls of colorful flowers on nearly every table. It was a hodgepodge of old and new, reflecting both their tastes, and even though they had the money now to do just about anything they wanted, signs of their earlier frugal life-style were still apparent everywhere. Like the old rocker Fanny refused to throw out, and the lacy curtains at the windows that were yellow with age. But they hadn't skimped when they'd decorated Peaches room, and it was a masterpiece in pink and white frills, and the room was filled with toys.

Expecting to find Peaches playing with her toys, or at the very least sulking, Jennifer was more than surprised, and concerned, to find her curled up on the bed, asleep.

"She must be exhausted," Jennifer said, joining the sisters in the kitchen a few minutes later. "I covered her, and she didn't budge."

Frances's eyes narrowed in thought. "Well, she didn't sleep much last night, that's for sure. She kept coming into my bedroom, wanting to climb into bed with me."

Fanny nodded. "And when she wasn't in Frances's room, she was in my room. Now, we all know she's scared of the dark, but we leave the lights on all the time, so that wasn't it.''

"Did you come straight home from the clinic yesterday?'' Jennifer asked.

Frances nodded. ''And little Peaches was fine. She'd settled down, and even ate supper. We played a few games, had a little sing-along, and then we went to bed.''

"And this morning?''

Fanny said, ''We got up with the chickens, just like we always do. When I went outside to do my chores, Peaches was in the kitchen with Frances.''

"But she didn't stay in the kitchen,'' Frances said. ''I went down in the cellar to get a jar of jam, and when I got back to the kitchen, she was gone. Next thing you know, she's up on the roof, screaming her head off. We tried everything we could to get her down, and that's when I called you.''

"How long were you in the cellar, Frances?''

"Maybe five minutes.''

"So whatever happened to upset her, happened in that length of time,'' Jennifer reasoned. ''I also think something fright-ened her. She was exhibiting a certain amount of agitation, of course, but I de-tected something else. A wild kind of ex-pression that suggests to me she was frightened.''

The sisters exchanged glances, and Fanny cleared her throat. ''Best we tell lit-tle Jennifer Gray about all the funny stuff that's been happenin', sister.''

''Funny stuff?''

Frances plopped down in a chair and sighed. ''Well, I admit we've had some strange goings-on, but I just know there's a logical explanation.''

Jennifer felt her heartbeat accelerate. ''Like what?''

Fanny waved a hand. ''Like missing food. A slice of pie here, part of a cake there, and at least a dozen cookies right out of the cookie jar. Frances thinks it was Peaches just being a bad girl, but it ain't like her to do things like that, so I think it's Frances's imagination a-workin' over-time. I think she's gettin' ticked in the head, and just forgot how many slices of pie were left, or how many cookies were in the cookie jar. Then, too, Frances has been hearin' footsteps at night, but I haven't, though I have to say I think we've had somebody in our garden, 'cause *I* sure didn't pull up all those radishes and green onions.''

Feeling the hair at the nape of her neck rise, Jennifer waited to hear Frances's retort, and prayed *both* of their imaginations were working overtime.

Frances cleared her throat. ''Well, there's no denying we've had some vegetables taken out of the garden, and we've both seen the light out in the barn at night, but—''

Jennifer broke in. ''It could've been a prowler! If you thought someone was out there, why didn't you call the sheriff?''

Fanny said, ''We called that nice Sheriff Cody the night we heard all that hammerin' in the cellar, and he came right out. But just between you and me, I think he thought we were both ticked in the head.''

''Where were you when you thought you heard hammering in the cellar?''

"In the living room," Frances said. "And we just stayed right there until the sheriff knocked on the door."

"Was Peaches with you?"

Frances nodded. "We told the sheriff about the night the chickens were raising a ruckus, too, and how our satchel got from the dining room into the living room all by itself, but I don't think he paid much attention. Though he did compliment us on all the nice things we've done to the house, and he even joined us for a cup of tea."

"Your satchel?"

"Uh-huh," Fanny said. "That big old satchel with the pretty flowers."

"When was the sheriff out here?" Jennifer asked.

"Last week," Frances replied.

"And have you had any more strange occurrences since he was here?"

Fanny shook her head.

Not wanting to alarm the sisters, but wondering now if there really was something sinister going on, and Peaches knew it, which might explain her odd behavior, Jennifer managed a smile. "Well, like you said, Frances, there must be a reasonable explanation. But I'll talk to the sheriff just the same. Meanwhile, try to keep Peaches calm, and give her all the love you can. And if you need me, I'm as close as a call.'' She pulled a business card out of her purse, and handed it to Frances. ''My pager number is written on the back, so if you can't reach me at the clinic or at home . . .''

''That's one of those little gadgets that beeps?'' Fanny asked.

''That's right, and I always have it with me. Now, I have to go. I won't make it back in time for church, but maybe I can catch the sheriff before he goes home.''

Frances gave Jennifer a hug. ''We want to thank you for helping us, Jennifer. You're a good friend.''

''You're very welcome. That little sweetie upstairs means a lot to me, too. Give her a hug for me when she wakes up?''

''Two hugs,'' Fanny said. ''One from each of us.''

The little house Jennifer shared with her grandfather and Emma was tucked in beside the Calico Christian Church, but far enough back to allow for an impressive garden that reached from the honeysuckle-covered porch to the street. A walkway leading from the street separated the garden. Wes grew vegetables on one side, and Emma grew flowers on the other, and during the hot summer months, they both enjoyed getting up at daybreak so they could work in the garden while it was cool.

And that was where Jennifer found them, talking to the sheriff and his wife. Emma was picking a bouquet of flowers, Wes was picking snap beans, and they were squabbling, as usual. This time, it was over the calories they'd consumed the night before, eating all that rich ice cream.

''I didn't twist your arm,'' Wes was saying.

''No, but you surely tempted me, bringing that wonderful strawberry ripple into the house.''

''I didn't bring it in,'' Wes teased. ''Blame Jennifer and Ken.''

''I can't do that when they aren't here to defend themselves.''

"Ah, but I'm here," Jennifer said, giving hugs around. "And I plead guilty. But wasn't it heavenly? Almost as heavenly as this gorgeous morning. Look at that sky. Yellow and pale pink meringue frosted with buttermilk."

"That's mighty poetic," Emma said.

Wes grinned. "And filled with calories. How did it go, sweetheart? Did you manage to get that little dickens down off the roof?"

"I did, but it wasn't easy. I'm really glad you're here, Sheriff. We have a lot to talk about."

Sheriff Jim Cody was a large, portly man with a head of thinning gray hair, and a warm smile. His wife, Ida, on the other hand, always looked like she'd just sucked on a sour lemon, and rarely had a good word about anyone, or the town of Calico. And today was no exception.

"I told Jim I think those two are getting ticky in the head," Ida said, "but then you never know. Like I told him, these days, you can't be too careful, and the ladies are living alone."

The sheriff cleared his throat. "I told Ida about all the odd things they claim have been happening, but I don't know, Jennifer. The Cromwell sisters have always had pretty vivid imaginations."

"What kind of things?" Emma asked.

Wes picked up the basket of snap beans, and nodded at the porch. "If we're going to have a long discussion about the Cromwell sisters, best we do it sitting on the porch, where we can enjoy a glass of iced tea and a little shade."

"What kind of things?" Emma repeated, after everybody was settled on the porch.

The sheriff spoke up. "They thought they heard hammering in the cellar one night, and called me. I went right out, but didn't find anything unusual. It was windy that night, and with that birch tree so close to the house, they probably heard tree branches hitting the roof."

"Maybe there was somebody in the basement, but he managed to get away before you arrived," Jennifer said thoughtfully. "The sisters said they were in the living room when they heard the noise, and stayed there until you knocked on the door. The culprit could have gone out the back door. They told me they've had some food missing, too, and somebody has been pulling up vegetables out of their garden.''

Emma's brows furrowed in thought. ''Missing food, vegetables out of the garden, and the sisters keep all the fruit and vegetables they put up in the cellar. Sounds like a hungry culprit to me.''

''Or maybe one who can't make ends meet, and enjoys supplementing his income by stealing,'' Jennifer reasoned. ''And that would certainly describe somebody who works for Elmer Dodd. That man still pays his employees peanuts. Have you heard of Charlie Biggs, Sheriff Cody?''

The sheriff frowned. ''Charlie Biggs. Nope, can't say I have.''

''He works at the dairy, and lives in one of the company cottages. I haven't seen him, but Ken says he is a large, rugged-looking man with white hair.''

Ida nodded her head. ''That sounds like the man I saw in the Mercantile the other day. He was flirting with Penelope Davis, and he had her so flustered, she couldn't remember if she had fifteen cats or fifty.''

Jennifer sighed. ''I'll bet Frances would love to hear that. Fanny says she's sweet on him.''

Ida rolled her eyes. ''Frances has a boyfriend? I'll bet Fanny loves that.''

''Well, I don't think Charlie Biggs is exactly a boyfriend, but no matter what their relationship is, Fanny has no room to talk, because she's sweet on Zacharias Hardy.''

''That's amazing,'' the sheriff said with a chuckle. ''Maybe Peaches is behaving badly because she's jealous.''

Jennifer replied, ''Maybe, or maybe she senses danger. Frances thinks Zacharias is after Fanny's money, and Fanny says the same thing about Charlie Biggs. Well, we know all about Zacharias. He's lived in Calico all his life, and his parents were born in Nebraska, but what do we know about Charlie Biggs? Maybe he's been prowling around the sisters' house looking for valuables and money, and simply took the food because it was available.''

''Well, I'll do some poking around and

see what I can turn up on this Charlie Biggs,'' the sheriff said. ''Only it can't be tomorrow. I'll be in court most of the morning, and then I have a doctor's appointment in the afternoon.''

''Nothing serious, I hope,'' Wes said.

''Nothing serious. Just my yearly physical, but it takes time to run all those tests.'' He gave Jennifer a sly smile. ''But that doesn't mean you can't do some poking around, young lady.''

''I know, and I'm going to. First thing in the morning, I'm going to go to the dairy and talk to Charlie Biggs. I know you're not supposed to judge a person by first impressions, but sometimes, it's the best way.''

Wes gave her a lopsided grin. ''And what are you going to do if you decide he's a gold-digging Romeo?''

''Then I'll tell Frances what I think, and advise her to be careful.''

''Boy oh boy, better you than me. That lady owns a shotgun, and she's a crack shot.''

Jennifer laughed. ''Well, that's better

than having to tell Fanny that Zacharias is a gold-digging Romeo. She has access to Frances's shotgun, and she can't hit the broad side of a barn. Seriously, Charlie Biggs might be totally innocent, but I think it's more than a little odd that the strange occurrences began about the same time Frances became interested in the man, and that warrants some sort of an investigation, don't you think?''

Wes said, ''I'd say it means you care a great deal for the sisters, and believe, like I do, that even though they are rough and tough, there is also a vulnerable side to them. But don't forget, to get to Charlie Biggs, you'll have to go through Elmer Dodd. And he might not take too kindly to pulling Biggs off the job so you can talk to him. You want me to tag along?''

''I can handle Elmer Dodd,'' Jennifer said, lifting her chin a notch. ''Besides, you're the one who said you're behind with the work on the bell tower, and why put off until tomorrow what you can do to-day?'' She gave Wes a hug. ''If I need help, I'll call Ken. I'm sure he'd be delighted to get the scoop, and take a lot of pictures, depicting Elmer as being less than cooperative.''

Wes grinned. ''Sounds like front-page stuff to me.''

Jennifer listened to them discuss Elmer Dodd, but her thoughts were on the Cromwell sisters and Peaches, and she could only hope and pray that there wouldn't be any more incidents between now and tomorrow morning.

Chapter Three

Although Elmer Dodd's dairy could hardly be called commanding, it had a certain charm about it, and part of it resembled a little town, where cottages had been built in a grove of elm trees for single employees. The cottages were issued on a first-come basis, with the exception of the resident vet, who lived in a trailer on the back of the property, overlooking the lion-colored open grazing land. At the moment, the resident vet was Elmer's nefarious nephew, Collin Dodd, who had planned to build a state-of-the-art animal hospital out near the new mall, thus hoping to put the Front Street Veterinary Clinic, and Jennifer and Ben, out of business. Fortunately, he hadn't been able to get the loan, and had to accept the job as resident vet.

The visitors' parking lot was on the road, adjacent to the company store, and Elmer's office was directly behind the store. Not a long distance, but it still took a good half hour by way of the store, and the crotchety, sullen clerk who had given Jennifer the third degree before he would even attempt to contact Elmer by phone, to tell him he had a visitor.

By the time Elmer finally ambled in through the side door, Jennifer was a bit annoyed. ''Do all your visitors get treated so graciously?'' she asked sarcastically.

Elmer was short and fat, with dark, slicked-back hair and yellow teeth. Dark beady eyes, too, and when he was out and about, he usually wore a cream-colored suit and a Panama hat. Now, he was wearing jeans and a plaid shirt, and hitched the jeans up a notch higher over his protruding belly. ''Don't usually have visitors during working hours,'' he muttered. ''And I don't like interruptions.''

Jennifer glanced at the scowling clerk. ''I'd like to talk to you in private, Mr. Dodd. If that's possible.''

He waved a hand. ''We can go to my office. Watch your step. Somebody left the hose on all night, and the ground is like a hog wallow.''

Glad she was wearing jeans and boots, Jennifer followed Elmer along the muddy pathway and into the small building behind the store.

''Excuse the clutter,'' he mumbled, moving an assortment of files from a chair. He lit a cigar, and sat down at his desk. ''You've got five minutes. What can I do for you?''

Determining the sugar approach would be much better than using vinegar, Jennifer sat down and managed a smile. ''Actually, I'd like to talk to you about one of your employees, and then if it's at all possible, I'd like to talk to him. His name is Charlie Biggs.''

Elmer's beady eyes narrowed. "What's old Charlie done now?"

"That's sounds like he's been in trouble before."

"So, he *is* in trouble."

"I didn't say that, Mr. Dodd. He's seeing quite a lot of Frances Cromwell, and because she's a good friend . . ."

"Uh-huh, well, he said something about that old bag, and I told him he was crazy."

Reminding herself that getting into an argument with the man wasn't going to get her anywhere, Jennifer gritted her teeth and pressed on. "How long has Charlie Biggs been working at the dairy?"

Elmer sighed. "Long enough for me to find out he's shiftless and lazy."

"And how long is that?"

"About four months. He came in from Omaha. No family."

"Has he ever been married?"

"Yeah, but his wife died. Probably died because she was married to him."

"Then I take it you don't care much for the man?"

Elmer shrugged. "He's personable

enough, but he doesn't like to work. Put him in charge of the milking machines, and he screwed everything up.''

''So what is he doing now?''

''Mucking out the barns. Running errands. Watering the plants and trees.'' He waved a hand. ''You saw his handiwork. He's the one who left the water running.''

''So why don't you fire him?''

''I would if I had somebody to take his place. But . . . well, see, he has this quality . . . Well, I don't know how to say it, except to say it. Everybody seems to think the cows give more milk when he's around. He sings a lot, see, and the cows listen.''

His comment brought a smile to Jennifer's face. ''Then he must have a nice singing voice.''

''I guess. Maybe he sings to Fanny Cromwell, and that's what turned her soft in the head.''

''It's Frances, not Fanny, and really, all I want to do is ask Charlie Biggs a few questions. Would it be possible to talk to him?''

Elmer shrugged again. ''I don't see why

not. You gonna ask him about his intentions?''

''Something like that. Fanny thinks he's a gold digger.''

And Jennifer's comment brought a smile to Elmer's face. ''Wouldn't be surprised. It's no secret he's down on his luck. You sit tight, and I'll see if I can round him up.''

Five minutes later, Elmer returned to the office with a tall, rugged-looking man who had the most beautiful silvery blue eyes Jennifer had ever seen. Snow white, wavy hair, too, and a wonderful smile. It was easy to see why Frances was attracted to the man, and why Penelope Davis had been so flustered.

Elmer introduced them, and then left them alone.

''I won't take much of your time, Mr. Biggs,'' Jennifer said easily. ''And I'll be honest. Frances Cromwell is a good friend of mine, and . . .''

Charlie chuckled. ''And you want to know about my intentions? That's really refreshing in this day and age, Miss Gray.

Frances is a very nice lady. I like her a lot.''

''How did you meet?''

''I was in the company store the day she came in to buy a tub of cottage cheese. Said it was for her chimp. Well, that took me back a bit, and one thing led to another.''

''You wanted to know about the chimp?''

Charlie sat on the edge of Elmer's desk, and nodded. ''You betcha. Wouldn't you? I mean, it's not every day of the week you're likely to find a chimpanzee in a town the size of Calico. She told me all about Peaches, and the next thing you know, she was inviting me to the house for lunch. Of course I didn't know she lived next door to the dairy at the time, or that she had a sister.''

''So did you go to their house for lunch?''

''I did. That's when I met the sister, Peaches, and the sister's boyfriend.''

''Are you talking about Zacharias Hardy?''

"Yeah, the old goat. Didn't like him then, and don't like him now."

"And why is that?" Jennifer asked.

"Because he keeps putting me down. All he does is talk about his farm, how high he can grow corn, and how he's known the Cromwell sisters for years. He sets out to make me feel like a loser and an intruder, and believe me, he knows just what buttons to push."

"Well, he *has* known the sisters for years, Mr. Biggs, so it's quite possible he was being protective of them, too."

"Yeah, well, with friends like that, you sure don't need enemies."

Jennifer managed another smile. "Do you mind answering a few questions?"

His response was immediate, and gentle. "Of course I don't mind. You obviously care a great deal for Frances, and I think that's great."

Jennifer relaxed. "Okay. Then you won't mind if the questions are a bit personal?"

"No, but why don't I make it easy for you, and give you a mini-résumé. I was

born and raised in Omaha, and that's where
I met and married my wife. And that's
where she died. I was working for Roland
Dodd, Elmer's brother, at the time, and he
was the one who told me about the opening
at the dairy. He said his no-account son,
Collin, was the dairy vet, and if he could
work for Elmer, anybody could. He knew
I wanted to make a change, and told me all
about Calico. It sounded like a good place
to live, and here I am.''

"And?"

"Are you asking me how I feel about
Frances? I like her. But I don't plan on getting married again, if that's what you're
getting at. I was married to the same wonderful woman for forty years, and I'd still
be married to her if she hadn't had that awful stroke. But I don't see anything wrong
with friendship, and it sure beats being
lonely.'' He eyed Jennifer intently. ''Elmer
said you're a vet. Do you own the Front
Street Veterinary Clinic?"

"I co-own it with my partner, Ben
Copeland. When was the last time you were
over at the Cromwell house, Mr. Biggs?"

Something unreadable flickered in his eyes. "Umm, last Tuesday, I think. I went over after my shift to sit a spell with Frances."

"Was Peaches there?"

"No, she was with Fanny, visiting that old goat across the road."

"So, when was the last time you saw Peaches?"

"The last time I had lunch with Frances. Guess that was about a week ago."

"And how did Peaches behave? Did she seem agitated?"

"She never sticks around long enough for me to tell if she's agitated or friendly. I walk in and she scampers away. Frances says she acts that way around the old goat across the road, too, so I shouldn't take it personally."

"You say you were working at Roland Dodd's meat-packing plant in Omaha when you found out about the job at the dairy. What kind of work did you do before that?"

"I owned a truck stop. You know. I sold gasoline, and had a little café where the truckers could get a meal and a cup of coffee. Made a good living, too, until the new highway went in, putting the truck stop about five miles off the route. Finally lost it to back taxes. Things went from bad to worse after that, along with my dreams for a comfortable retirement, because I was too old to start over.''

''That's a very pessimistic attitude, Mr. Biggs.''

Charlie shrugged. ''We live in a pessimistic world. That's why when a little bit of happiness comes along, you grab it.''

''You mean like your friendship with Frances Cromwell?''

''Among other things.'' He smiled at Jennifer. ''I wouldn't worry about Frances, Miss Gray. She's a strong lady.''

''Yes, she is, until it comes to affairs of the heart. I think she could get hurt very easily.''

''And you're here today to make sure that doesn't happen? Well, I can assure you, it won't. I've been honest with Frances from the beginning, and she knows exactly how I feel.''

Jennifer stood up. "I'm glad. Thanks for talking to me, Mr. Biggs."

He stood up as well, and the smile widened. "The pleasure was all mine."

Frances was out front watering when Jennifer pulled up the long gravel driveway, and she could tell there hadn't been any more incidents by the smile on the woman's face.

"Well, this is a surprise." Frances beamed. "Didn't expect to see you again so soon."

"Just wanted to check on Peaches before I head for the clinic," Jennifer said, getting out of the Jeep. "Where is she?"

"In the house with Fanny. Fanny is cooking up a batch of pancakes because we're both mighty hungry this morning."

"Then you had a good night?"

"Slept like babies. Even Peaches, and she stayed in her room all night." She waved a hand at the flower bed in front of the house. "We could give Emma a run with them flowers, don't you think?"

The bed was a hodgepodge of purple

asters, yellow and orange marigolds, dahlias, pink petunias, and white daisies, and it was gorgeous. "Yes, you certainly could. I'd like to see Peaches, but I can only stay a minute."

"Then you go right on in, and tell Fanny I'll be along as soon as I finish watering."

Jennifer walked through the living room that smelled like lemon polish, and into the sun-splashed kitchen. Peaches let out a squeal, and raised her arms for a hug.

"Well, now," Fanny said. "This is a surprise. Well, you don't have to worry about Peaches none. She had a good night."

"That's what Frances said," Jennifer said, sitting down at the table. Peaches was in her lap, with her long arms wrapped around Jennifer's neck again, but this time it wasn't for comfort, only affection. She was still in her pajamas, and Jennifer hugged her close.

"Frances wanted to do the outside chores this mornin', but that was okay with me, 'cause I like my pancakes better than hers. Will you join us for breakfast, Jennifer?''

The aroma of the pancakes cooking on the griddle was wonderful, and Jennifer's stomach growled with hunger. "I was only going to stay a minute, but how can I resist! I'd like that very much, Fanny."

Fanny clucked her tongue. "Well, we was gonna use just butter and some applesauce for the topping, but now that we've got us a special guest, I think we should use some of Frances's special syrup. Only thing is, it's down in the cellar. If you'd go get it for me, I'd be most appreciative, little Jennifer. It's in a flowered jar a-sittin' to the right of my strawberry jam. The jar is marked, too, so you can't miss it."

Jennifer put the chimp in a chair, and gave her another hug. "You sit there like a good girl, sweetie, and I'll be right back."

The door to the cellar was off the kitchen, and Jennifer had just reached for the handle when Peaches began shrieking and jumping up and down on the chair.

Fanny exclaimed, "What on earth!"

Jennifer returned to the table, and held Peaches close.

The ruckus brought Frances on the run, too, and the concern on her face was undeniable.

Jennifer shook her head. ''I don't know what to say, Frances. Everything was fine until I headed for the cellar to get a jar of syrup. And now I can't help but wonder if the cellar has something to do with what happened yesterday. You said you were down in the cellar for five minutes, Frances, and when you came up, Peaches was up on the roof screeching. And that tells me Peaches doesn't want *anybody* to go down in the cellar. Did the sheriff check out the cellar when he was here that night?''

Frances said, ''He did, but we didn't go with him.''

Peaches was clinging to Jennifer again, and shivering. ''Frances, I want you to take Peaches to her room, and keep her there while I look around in the you-know-what.''

Fanny added four pancakes to the stack,

and frowned. "You think there is something down in the you-know-what?"

"I don't know, but I think Peaches
thinks there is. I'll need a flashlight. . . ."

Frances quickly left the room with
Peaches, and after handing Jennifer a flashlight, Fanny began to scowl. "You be careful, little Jennifer Gray. Those steps are
mighty steep. The light switch is right
there. Ain't the best light in the world, but
at least you can see enough to get down the
stairs."

Jennifer turned on the switch, and
headed down the rickety stairs. The musty
cellar contained the furnace, rows of stor-
age boxes, and two walls lined with
shelves. And the shelves were filled with
jams, jellies, and preserved vegetables.

Gunnysacks filled with potatoes, onions,
and turnips lined the far wall, and above
them was the sloping outside cellar door.
The sisters had said they heard hammering
that night, but it wasn't until Jennifer ex-
amined the door that she realized what the
intruder had done. He had taken off the

lock, which meant he could have access to the cellar anytime he wanted.

Chilled to the bone, Jennifer looked for the syrup, couldn't find it, and quickly climbed the stairs. In the kitchen again, she called out to Frances, and took a ragged breath.

"I left Peaches in her room," Frances said, hurrying into the kitchen. "Uh-oh, I don't like the look on your face, little Jennifer Gray."

"And I don't like what I'm thinking," Jennifer returned. "I don't see a lock on the door to the basement."

"Never thought we needed one," Fanny replied. "We got us a lock on the outside cellar door."

"You don't anymore. The lock is gone. I think the intruder removed it, and that's what you heard that night. It also means the intruder has had access to your basement the whole time, and without the door to the kitchen locked, he's had access to the house, too. And I think Peaches knows it, which would account for her odd behavior."

Fanny sucked in her breath. ''Why, we could've gotten killed in our beds!''

''I couldn't find the syrup,'' Jennifer said.

Frances took the flashlight and headed down the stairs. And when she returned to the kitchen, her face was ashen. ''The jar of syrup is gone, sister, along with a couple of jars of cider, the honey we got from Mr. Babkins, and three bottles of elixir.''

Jennifer hurried to the wall phone, and dialed the sheriff's number. And this time, there was no way he could accuse the sisters of having overactive imaginations. Somebody had gone to a lot of trouble to gain access to the sisters' house, and just the thought of it was terrifying!

Chapter Four

"Drink your tea, sweetheart," Wes encouraged. "It will help settle your nerves."

Jennifer, Wes, and Emma were sitting at the table in their bright, sunny kitchen, but the mood was far from cheery. "I don't know if I can get it down," Jennifer returned. "It's like I've got this big, sick lump in my throat, and I can hardly swallow."

Emma muttered, "Well, I can understand that. Nothing is going to settle my nerves, either, until the sheriff calls and tells us that little house is safe and secure."

"I'm not so sure we'll be able to relax then," Wes said thoughtfully. "The whole thing is pretty scary, and makes you wonder what this world is coming to. Admittedly, those ladies have some money in the bank now, but all you have to do is look around their house to know they still live conservatively. So what's to take? A bag of potatoes? A few onions and radishes out of the garden? A couple of bottles of elixir? A jar of honey they bought or bartered from Mr. Babkins? A jar of Fanny's special syrup? They don't own a piece of jewelry between them, except for those old brooches they always wear on their dresses and their pocket watches, and there isn't a speck of china, crystal, or silver in the house."

Emma nodded. "And they probably wouldn't get fifty dollars for all their doodads at a rummage sale, and you'd surely need a forklift and a truck to cart away all that heavy furniture."

Jennifer had gone to the clinic after the sheriff arrived at the Cromwell house, but she'd been so upset, Ben told her to go home. Now she had a king-size headache, and couldn't shake the feeling they were headed in the wrong direction. "Maybe the intruder wasn't there to a burglarize the house," she said finally. "The sisters were raised by their father and their Uncle Mitford, and everybody knows they were bootlegging men. Maybe they hid money somewhere in the house and somebody knows about it, and is trying to find it."

"Or maybe somebody is trying to scare the sisters off," Wes said thoughtfully.

Jennifer groaned. "Like Elmer Dodd. He'll never get over the fact he had to give the sisters all that money for the ten acres his father took from the Cromwell men illegally, but I don't know, Grandfather. Elmer isn't a very nice man, but I just can't see him going that far."

"I can't either," Emma said. "What's done is done, and he would have nothing to gain. I'm more inclined to agree with you, Jennifer. There is something in that house the culprit wants, something that has been there all this time, and I have the feeling a truckload of locks won't keep the culprit out if he has a notion to get in.''

Wes shook his head. ''Now, that's one scary thought.''

Jennifer ran a hand over her tired eyes. ''When I left, Frances was loading her shotgun. And I know she wouldn't hesitate to use it. Old Charlie and Zacharias had better go in waving a white flag.''

Wes drummed his fingers on the table. ''You know, maybe that's the answer. Let the men stand guard. One of them one night, one the next. It seems to me if they care for the sisters, they would want to help. You said Charlie is a large, rugged man, and Zacharias is a good-sized man, too. Sounds to me like they could handle themselves if they came face-to-face with the intruder.''

Jennifer sighed. ''It's a thought, but I don't know how well they would work together.''

''But they wouldn't be working together.''

''No, but they'd have to get together to make their plans, and from what Charlie said, that might be a problem. Charlie doesn't like Zacharias, and I have the feeling it's mutual.''

''Did Charlie say why he doesn't like Zacharias?'' Emma asked.

''He said Zacharias deliberately tries to make him feel like he's a loser, or words to that effect. Charlie calls Zacharias an old goat.''

Emma tittered. ''Well, at least he calls 'em as he sees 'em. Zacharias Hardy *is* an old goat, and he can be just about as nasty as one, too. I'll never forget the time he was in the Mercantile trying to buy a pair of work shoes, and jumped all over the clerk because they didn't have his size. He had the poor girl in tears.''

Wes nodded. ''If you go back far enough, I think he's had a row with just about everybody in town at one time or another. He was a lot more agreeable when his wife was still alive.''

Emma snorted. ''Well, after Geneva died, you didn't turn into a tyrant, Wes.''

Wes gave Emma a mischievous grin. ''That's because I had you to keep me in line. Seriously, maybe the sheriff should put a deputy on the house for a while.''

Jennifer returned, ''I don't know, Grandfather. There are only eight deputies, and the sheriff is always complaining because he doesn't have enough men to cover the county. Maybe I should spend a few days with the sisters.''

Emma harrumphed. ''Well, I don't like that idea one bit. Besides, if the culprit knows you're there, he'll just back off until you leave. What's that going to prove, or how is that going to catch him?'' She sighed. ''Guess the same thing would apply, no matter who is standing guard.''

A few minutes later, the sheriff arrived, and he looked as weary as they felt.

''I was going to call, but decided to stop by instead,'' he said, taking a seat at the table. ''And if you have any more of that tea, I could surely use a cup, Emma.''

''How are the sisters holding up?'' Jennifer asked.

''Not too good, and Peaches senses all the tension, so she's acting up again. I got the lock installed on the outside cellar door, and a lock put on the kitchen door to the cellar. Dusted for fingerprints, too. Haven't been able to do a comparison test yet, but just by the field test, I'd say there weren't any that didn't belong there.''

Wes said, ''Which means the intruder was wearing gloves.''

''That's what I think.''

Emma placed a cup of tea in front of the sheriff. ''Jennifer was just saying a few minutes ago that maybe the Cromwell men stashed something in the house before they died, the culprit knows about it, and that's what he's looking for.''

The sheriff shrugged. ''Like money? They were bootlegging men, so that's a possibility, but if we decided to investigate that angle, it would mean we'd have to take the house apart board by board.''

''Boy oh boy, the sisters wouldn't stand for that.''

''No, they wouldn't, Wes, and I sure wouldn't want to broach the subject, would you?''

Wes said, ''No, I wouldn't. So what happens now?''

"The sisters are gonna take turns sitting up all night. And I told them to call me if they so much as hear a squeak.

"Now, I've gotta go home, and tell my wife I didn't keep my doctor's appointment this afternoon, and believe me, I'm not looking forward to the fallout. She'll rant and rave for hours. Thanks for the tea, Emma."

Jennifer walked with the sheriff to the door, and said, "Did Charlie Biggs or Zacharias Hardy show up this afternoon?"

"Nope, they sure didn't. And just between us, I think the ladies could've used their support. Try to get some rest, Jennifer. You looked whipped."

"You heard the sheriff," Emma said, after the door closed behind him. "Go get some rest. I'll wake you up when supper is ready."

Jennifer shook her head. "I have too much on my mind to sleep. You know a lot about the remodeling that had to be done before the sisters could move back into the old house, Grandfather."

Emma smiled. "That's because your

grandaddy is mighty handy with a hammer and nails. The sisters knew he helped build this house, and they wanted his expert opinion.''

''Well, I don't know how expert my opinion was,'' Wes said, ''but I was willing to help them as much as I could.''

''I know they had to put on a new roof and repair some flooring and the banister on the inside staircase, but what else was done?''

''That was about all, sweetheart. The house hadn't been lived in for five years, so it looked a lot worse than it was. They had to do a lot of cleaning, of course, and paint all the rooms, and repair the mantel over the fireplace, but all in all, the house was pretty sound.''

''So, if the Cromwell men had hidden away a cache of money, it might not have been uncovered during the remodeling.''

Emma wearily shook her head. ''Do you know how many places you could hide money or valuables in an old house like that?''

''Reminds me of the time my daddy and

mama bought the old house out on Willow Road after the lady who owned it died,'' Wes said. ''We had been living closer to town, but my daddy wanted some room to plant a garden. The house isn't there anymore, but I'll never forget what a delight it was. I was only ten years old, and every musty old room was a treat. We'd been living there about a month or so, when I heard the rumors. Seems the old lady who owned the house didn't trust banks, and supposedly kept her money hidden somewhere in the house. My mama and daddy didn't believe it, but I did, and I spent nearly all summer looking for false walls and floorboards. Even checked every brick in the fireplace. Never did find anything, but I still think that old house was torn down with the treasure somewhere inside.''

Emma snorted. ''And he talks about *my* imagination!''

Jennifer got up and stretched. ''If I have time before supper, I'd like to take a walk along the river.''

''You have plenty of time,'' Emma said. ''With everything that's been going on, I forgot to get the chicken out of the freezer. Now I have to defrost it in the microwave, and figure out what to do with it. And that's a sorry state of affairs, what with Ken Hering coming for supper.''

Jennifer raised a brow. ''You didn't tell me Ken was coming for supper.''

''Well, honey, with everything going on, it clean slipped my mind.''

A flush swept Jennifer's cheeks. ''Well, I guess I'll go upstairs and freshen up and save the walk for another day.''

Emma and Wes exchanged winks and smiles as Jennifer hurried out of the room.

There had been many, many times since she'd come home from veterinary school when Jennifer had driven along Calico's dark, lonely streets in the middle of the night, after receiving an emergency call from Ben. But the call this time had come from Frances Cromwell, and it wasn't only an emergency, it was a nightmare! It had been Fanny's turn to keep watch, and at a little after 4:00 A.M., she'd gone upstairs to check on Peaches, and discovered she was missing.

"You okay?" Wes said, giving Jennifer's shoulder a squeeze. "I know, that's a dumb question. Did Frances say if the bedroom window was open?"

"No, she didn't. She was nearly hysterical, Grandfather. I told her to call the sheriff, and that we were on our way. I know Peaches has been upset, but I didn't expect her to run away! I should have brought her home with me yesterday. If I had . . ."

"You can't blame yourself," Wes said. "Nor is it all that easy to outthink a chimp, especially a chimp that's as bright as Peaches. Kids usually run away from home because they're unhappy, and Peaches is just like a little kid, and we all know how upset she's been."

Jennifer sighed. "She could be anywhere, Grandfather. And it won't be light for at least another hour . . ." She broke off, and tried to swallow the tears clogging her throat.

*   *   *

Jennifer made it to the Cromwell house in record time, and breathed a sigh of relief when she saw the sheriff's car and a patrol car in the driveway.

"I know," Wes said, climbing out of the Jeep. "The more people we have searching the area, the better."

The sheriff opened the front door before they knocked, and said, "I'm sure glad to see you two." He waved a hand toward the kitchen. "The sisters are in quite a state."

"Have you looked for Peaches?" Jennifer asked, hurrying into the kitchen.

"Not yet," the sheriff said, loping along behind her. "We just got here, for one thing, and right now we're trying to establish what happened."

"I'll tell you what happened!" Frances exclaimed tearfully. "Peaches ran away from home!"

Wearing old flannel robes, the sisters were sitting at the kitchen table, with a box of tissues between them, and the sight of their tear-streaked faces twisted Jennifer's heart. Deputy Manny Pressman, a stocky, friendly man, sat at the table with them, jotting things down in a notepad.

Fanny looked up. "Well, we're mighty glad to see you, little Jennifer Gray, and we're might glad to see your nice grand-daddy, too."

Jennifer put water on for tea, and took the deputy's place at the table. Wes was already sitting across from Frances, and held her hand.

Deputy Pressman leaned against the counter, and looked at his notes. "Fanny says she went upstairs to check on Peaches, and—"

"And she was gone!" Fanny sobbed. "I woke up Frances right away, and we looked all over the house."

Frances bobbed her head. "Peaches was agitated when she went to bed, so we thought she might be hiding."

"Was the bedroom window open?" Jennifer asked.

Fanny nodded. "The bedrooms are up-stairs, so we always keep 'em open a crack on hot summer nights."

"And was the window still cracked when you went into the bedroom?"

"No, it was wide open, but Peaches wouldn't go out into the night. She's scared of the dark."

Wes asked, "Could Peaches get the window open wider by herself?"

Frances shrugged. "She's strong, but I've never seen her open a window."

"What happened after the sheriff left yesterday afternoon?" Jennifer asked.

Frances shrugged again. "Not much. Charlie Biggs came by with a tub of cottage cheese for Peaches, and not more than five minutes after he left, Zacharias came over, wanting Fanny to have supper with him."

"But I didn't go," Fanny said. "Peaches was acting up, and I didn't want to leave her."

"How was she acting up?" Wes asked.

Fanny blew her nose. "She was sulking, mostly. Wouldn't eat her supper, neither. Frances turned the radio on and got some nice music, but that didn't do much good."

The deputy looked at his watch. "We're

gonna wait until it's light to begin the search, because we sure don't want to be tramping around and messing up the clues.''

The sheriff nodded. "Frances says they had the sprinklers going late yesterday afternoon, so we might be able to see Peaches's footprints.''

Jennifer asked, "Did you hear anything suspicious before you went to check on Peaches, Fanny?''

Fanny lowered her eyes. "No, 'cause I was dozing on the couch.''

"Can Peaches open doors?'' the sheriff asked.

"She can open doors,'' Frances replied, "and if Fanny was dozing on the couch . . .''

Tears filled Fanny's eyes. "I know, sister. You don't have to say it. 'Twas my fault.''

Frances reached over and gave Fanny a hug. "I'm not blaming you, sister. We've got us a set of circumstances here, and there isn't much we can do about it. And even if she did open the front door, why would she go out in the dark?''

When the water was hot, Jennifer made the tea, while Wes asked question after question, concentrating mostly on the outbuildings on the property. There weren't many, but any one of them could be a potential hiding place.

''We'll spread out as soon as it's light,'' the sheriff said. ''But I want the sisters to stay right here, in the event Peaches is hiding someplace in the house that nobody knows about. Jennifer, you take the front and the immediate area around the house. Manny, you take the fenceline alongside the dairy, all the way from the road to the back of the property. Wes and I will take the outbuildings, and the property line to the east. If anybody sees anything even remotely suspicious, yell.''

''What color pajamas was Peaches wearing?'' Jennifer asked.

Tears rolled down Fanny's cheeks. ''Yellow. Made 'em just last week from that bolt of material we got from the Mercantile. Got enough left to make her a play-

suit and a little pinafore, too, and some
aprons for us. . . . She's so scared of the
dark, Jennifer. I just know she ain't out
there, a-wandering around.''

Jennifer forced a smile. ''I have the feeling we'll find her in one of the outbuildings, and in no time at all, she'll be right
here in the kitchen, chattering, making
faces, and wanting to give mushy kisses to
tell you how sorry she is.''

Jennifer's words sounded hollow, but the
sisters' faces brightened. And that was all
that mattered, because without hope they
had nothing at all.

The sky was lemon yellow by the time
Jennifer had covered the front yard and one
side of the house. And the sheriff had been
right. The ground was damp, but there were
no signs of the chimp. Nor had she heard
any yells or whistles, which meant the men
hadn't had any luck, either.

Downhearted, Jennifer made her way
around to the other side of the house, and
looked up at Peaches's open window. Directly below it, the eaves slanted down to

a low overhang. Concluding it wouldn't have taken much for the chimp to slide down the overhang and drop to the ground, Jennifer looked down, and found herself holding her breath. The damp ground was trampled in several spots, but even more curious, there were two deep indentations in the ground that were approximately two feet apart. Like a ladder had been placed against the sloping eaves.

Trying to grasp what the discovery meant, but finding it very hard to believe Peaches had actually been abducted, Jennifer hurried to the corner of the house, and whistled through her teeth.

Chapter Five

"Well, if that isn't the ticket!" Emma exclaimed. "Why, who would've thought it? Little Peaches kidnapped? I can hardly believe it!"

Jennifer was on the kitchen phone with Emma, and lowered her voice. "The sisters are in the living room with the sheriff, Emma, but I'm still going to keep my voice down, because I don't want them to hear me say this. Well, it's possible it was an abduction, not a kidnapping. . . ."

Emma snorted. "And there's a difference?"

"There could be a big difference. A kidnapping usually means the kidnapper wants something in return."

"Like money? Then it would have to be somebody who knows the sisters got all that money from Elmer Dodd."

"That's right, and that just about covers the whole town, because there was a lot of publicity at the time."

"I remember. They even had a picture in the newspaper of Elmer handing the check to the sisters." Emma cleared her throat. "And if little Peaches was abducted?"

"That's even scarier, Emma, because there are a lot of unscrupulous people out there, who make a business out of snatching up animals for laboratory experiments. You read about it all the time, and I would think a chimp like Peaches would be a real prize."

Emma sucked in her breath. "Good heavens, that's terrible!"

"Yes, it is. And just like the money they received from Elmer Dodd, almost everybody in town knows the sisters have the chimp. I know, it's frightening to think we might have somebody like that living in Calico, but we can't count it out.''

''And you say you found the imprints of a ladder in the mud underneath Peaches's bedroom window?''

''That's right. The sisters have one ladder they keep in the toolshed, and the shed is always unlocked, but that wasn't the ladder the culprit used. The sheriff already checked it for mud. There were a lot of footprints in the mud, too, but nothing clear enough to get a casting. The lawn begins about a foot away, so there was no way to follow a trail, even if there was one. We have to believe the culprit used the ladder to get up on the eaves. From there, it was only a matter of crawling the rest of the way, opening the window wider, and coaxing Peaches out, though that part of it is the real mystery, because the sisters claim Peaches would never have gone outside in the middle of the night willingly, because she's afraid of the dark.''

''The sisters didn't hear her put up a fuss?''

"Frances was asleep, and Fanny says she was dozing on the couch, so either that was the reason they didn't hear anything, or Peaches went willingly, or . . ."

"Terrible," Emma uttered. "Has the sheriff called the FBI?"

"He called the field office in Lincoln, but they said they couldn't help us. Peaches is a chimp, Emma, so I'm afraid we're on our own, at least until we can find out what actually happened to her."

"Well, she's an important chimp, and if that man is going to demand money . . ."

"But we don't know if that's his plan. If he does, they said they'll have an agent look into it.

"Now, I have to go, Emma, but I'll keep in touch."

"I take it you're going to stay with the sisters?"

"I'll stay as long as they need me."

"They must be devastated."

"They are, and it's so sad, I can hardly stand it. I called the clinic, so Ben knows what's going on, and Ken is on his way out. We all agree the more media coverage we can get on this, the better.''

Emma's voice quavered. ''What can I do, honey?''

''Pack an overnight case for me. Underwear, nightclothes, a pair of shorts, a blouse, and toiletries. Grandfather is on his way home now to pick it up. And you can pray, Emma. Pray it's a kidnapping, the kidnapper wants money, and has no intentions of harming Peaches.''

Emma's reply was barely a whisper. ''I'll pray harder than I ever prayed in my life.''

By the time Jennifer joined the sheriff and the sisters in the living room, Ken had arrived, and she went straight into his arms.

Ken held her tenderly for a few minutes before he cleared his throat and said, ''I stopped by the radio station, and they're going to broadcast a description of Peaches every half hour, beginning at noon. And John, Jr., is holding a spot on the front page for tomorrow's edition.'' He gave Jennifer a hug, and sat down on the couch beside the sisters. ''What I'd like to do is get a picture of Peaches's room, and then one from the outside, and the open window. I'd also like a photo of Peaches, if you have one.''

Fanny wiped her eyes, and her chin trembled. ''We took some pictures of her just last week, and took the film out to that place in the mall to get 'em developed real quick. The envelope is right over there on the table.''

''She was wearing a new blue pinafore,'' Frances mumbled. ''Had a blue bow in her hair, too.''

The sheriff said, ''It might not hurt to take some snaps of the eaves and the ground underneath with all the scuffed-up footprints, either.''

Ken nodded. ''Will do, and then I'd like to get the story in detail, so there won't be any mistakes in the paper.''

Jennifer hadn't been up to Peaches's bedroom since she'd disappeared, and the sheriff noted the pain in her eyes. ''I'll take Ken up, Jennifer. Meanwhile, maybe you can make some tea?''

They had tried several times over the

course of the morning to get the sisters to
drink a cup of tea, but to no avail. And
Fanny was shaking her head again. ''Don't
want no tea, but I wouldn't mind havin' a
glass of elixir.''

''I'd like a glass, too,'' Frances said.
''Have a jarful in the kitchen, right there in
the cupboard next to the stove.''

Thinking maybe they all needed a glass
of the sisters' famous elixir, Jennifer
headed for the kitchen.

By two o'clock that afternoon, the radio
station had broadcast the news of Peaches's
abduction five times, and the phone was
ringing off the hook. Alone with the sisters
now, Jennifer took every call seriously,
thanking the citizens who wanted to pay
their respects, and writing down the names
and phone numbers of the callers who
claimed to have seen Peaches. But she
didn't have much faith in those calls after
one woman admitted she'd probably seen a
brown shaggy dog, and one man admitted
he couldn't see beyond the end of his nose
in broad daylight.

At two-thirty, Zacharias Hardy arrived, carrying a bouquet of yellow roses. He was tall and rangy, with sharp features, a head of steel gray hair, and dark brown, piercing eyes. Because he always had a scowl on his weathered face, Jennifer found him to be a bit intimidating, to say the least, and could easily see why Charlie Biggs didn't like him. But Fanny was so glad to see him, she actually smiled, and it *had* been very sweet of him to bring her the bouquet of roses.

''So you're the pastor's granddaughter, huh?'' Zacharias said, looking down his nose at Jennifer. ''I haven't seen you since you were about *that* big.'' He waved a hand downward. ''That was when my Edith was alive, and we used to go to church all the time.''

''Hello, Mr. Hardy,'' Jennifer said, working at a smile.

He handed her the roses. ''You might as well put 'em in water. Don't look like Fanny intends on getting up off the couch.''

The sisters were wearing coveralls now,

and Fanny stuffed her hands in her pockets. "Every time I get up I feel dizzy, so I figured this is the safest place to be."

"And I feel a little woozy, too," Frances said. "We both are so thankful for little Jennifer Gray's help."

"I'll put the roses in water," Jennifer said, heading for the kitchen.

Surprised when Zacharias followed her, Jennifer managed another smile. "The roses are lovely. Did they come from your garden?"

"No," he snapped. "I walked down the road and swiped them out of Joe Greely's garden. Of course they are from my garden! You want to tell me why Fanny and Frances are soused at two o'clock in the afternoon? I can smell 'em from five feet away, and neither one of them could focus their eyes on a barn wall painted fire-engine red."

Jennifer pulled a vase out of the cupboard, and gritted her teeth. "I don't think you understand what is happening here, Mr. Hardy. Peaches was either kidnapped or abducted, and to the sisters it's like losing a child.''

''Yeah, well, I heard the news broadcast, and if you ask me, it's the best thing that's happened to them in years, other than maybe getting the old homestead back from that crooked Elmer Dodd. I've been telling them ever since they moved in, they'd be better off to get rid of that monkey and get a cow. At least they'd get milk from a cow, instead of grief. All that monkey gives them is grief.''

''Peaches isn't a monkey, Mr. Hardy, she's an ape.''

Zacharias shrugged. ''What's the difference? I want to take Fanny somewhere, or fix her a nice dinner over at my house, and she won't leave because the blasted monkey is acting up.''

''Haven't you ever had a pet?'' Jennifer asked the obnoxious man.

''Sure. Lots of 'em over the years. Dogs that watched my property, and cats that killed rats and mice. At least they earned their keep.''

"Then you don't think companionship and love count for anything?"

"Sure I do, and that's what I keep trying to give Fanny."

"If you mean that, try to have a little compassion, too, Mr. Hardy. Try to be like the rest of the town."

His eyes narrowed. "Meaning?"

"People have been calling all afternoon wanting to give Frances and Fanny their support."

His eyes were slits now. "And if the kidnapper calls, how is he gonna get through if the line is all tied up?"

Jennifer sighed. "I didn't think of that, so I guess I'd better do something about it."

"You gonna rip out the phone? Lot of good that would do. Then the kidnapper couldn't get through at all."

"No, I'm not going to rip out the phone. I'm going to call a friend of mine who works for *The Calico Review*, and have him get in touch with the radio station. Maybe they can make a special announcement that will slow down the calls. And as far as the sisters being a little tipsy at two o'clock in the afternoon, I guess that's my fault. All they've wanted to do is drink their elixir, and . . .''

Zacharias threw his head back and laughed. "Elixir? Why don't you call it what it is, Miss Gray? Rotgut moonshine. That's what killed their old man and their Uncle Mitford, you know.'' He opened the refrigerator and took out a dozen eggs. ''You go tell those ladies that I'm fixing 'em eggs and flapjacks, and they are gonna eat every bite.''

Jennifer opened her mouth and closed it, and carried the roses into the living room. ''Zacharias is fixing eggs and flapjacks,'' she repeated, ''and he says you have to eat every bite.''

Fanny gave Jennifer a wan smile. "Eggs and flapjacks don't sound too bad.''

''Sounds terrible,'' Frances muttered, but she didn't protest beyond that.

By three-thirty, the sisters had eaten fair-sized portions of scrambled eggs and flapjacks, and while Zacharias kept them company in the living room, Jennifer cleaned up the mess in the kitchen. Thinking that his slovenliness was probably the reason why he wanted a woman in his life, she was banging around the pots and pans, when a light tap sounded at the back door.

It was Charlie Biggs, and he was carrying a bouquet of daisies. "D-don't want to be no bother here," he said hesitantly, "but I just heard the broadcast on the radio. I was going to call, but the guy on the radio said everybody should curtail the calls to keep the phone line clear, in case . . ." He took a deep breath. "I can't believe somebody kidnapped little Peaches!"

Jennifer sighed. "Well, we don't know that it was an actual kidnapping, Mr. Biggs. Of course, if we get a call demanding money, we'll have our answer."

He handed Jennifer the flowers. "Is Frances okay?"

"Not really, and that's why I'm here. Both Frances and Fanny are going to need some help to get through this."

"Did they call the sheriff?"

"Yes, and the sheriff is doing all he can."

"You suppose I can see Frances?"

"I don't know why not. Zacharias Hardy is visiting Fanny."

Charlie groaned. "Wonderful. Maybe I'd better come back later."

Jennifer had the daisies in a vase, and handed it to him. "She needs you right now, Mr. Biggs. Take her the bouquet, smile a lot, and ignore that offensive twit."

Charlie chuckled low in his throat. "You mean Zacharias?"

"None other. If you need help, holler."

Charlie looked around the kitchen. "You know, I don't think I've ever seen the sisters' kitchen in a clutter like this."

"You should have seen it ten minutes ago," Jennifer replied testily. "Zacharias fixed eggs and flapjacks for the sisters, and apparently keeping things neat isn't his style."

"Wouldn't turn that old goat loose in *my* kitchen," Charlie muttered, heading for the living room.

And almost immediately, a voice rose.

"What's the matter, Biggs?" Zacharias said with a snarl. "Is that the best you can do?"

"Nothing wrong with a bouquet of daisies," Charlie returned. "And at least I had the decency to change into clean clothes before I came calling."

"You suggesting my clothes are dirty?" came Zacharias's angry reply.

Jennifer hurried into the living room, and announced, "If the two of you can't keep a civil tongue in your heads, I think you'd better leave!"

Charlie looked at her sheepishly. "I didn't come here to cause a hassle, Miss Gray, but I'm not about to stand here and let Hardy put me down. Not today. Not ever again. I came to be with Frances during this trying time, and—"

At that moment, Jennifer saw Wes's dark blue sedan pull up the driveway, and broke in. "My grandfather is here, so I suggest you both save your excuses for him. He's a very good mediator, by the way, and won't put up with nonsense, so you had better be prepared." Jennifer peered through the window, and was surprised, though delighted, to see Emma getting out of the car, too.

Jennifer met them at the door with hugs, and whispered, "Zacharias Hardy and Charlie Biggs are in the living room with the sisters, and they've already had a tiff. I was telling them I thought they should leave when you drove up."

Emma pursed her lips. "Well, I'll put 'em both to work. We have the car full of groceries, and a few dishes I managed to put together this morning."

At that point, Emma marched into the living room, said hello to the sisters and Zacharias, introduced herself to Charlie Biggs, and began handing out orders. Charlie didn't mind, but Zacharias did, and left, muttering something about having to go home to feed the chickens.

"Good riddance," Jennifer whispered, giving Wes's hand a squeeze.

After the grocery bags and food had been carried into the kitchen, Wes and Charlie kept the sisters company in the living room while Jennifer and Emma put away the groceries.

"Have the sisters eaten anything today?" Emma asked, taking inventory of the things in the refrigerator.

"Scrambled eggs and flapjacks. Zacharias cooked, and I cleaned up after him."

Emma frowned. "That old goat. Bet his scrambled eggs taste like sawdust, and his flapjacks would make good Frisbees. But I must say, Charlie Biggs seems like a very nice man."

"He is, when he isn't around Zacharias. Except for Fanny, that man seems to bring out the worst in everybody."

A few minutes later, Charlie plodded into the kitchen, and his shoulders were slumped. "Those two are taking this pretty bad. I'm glad the pastor is here." He heaved a big sigh. "I have some watering to do over at the dairy, but I made Frances promise to call if she needs me."

"You said that man doesn't have matrimony in mind," Emma said after Charlie had gone. "But he surely seems to care for Frances."

"And in his own way, I think Zacharias cares for Fanny, too, but having those two men in the same room together is like mixing oil and water, and right about now, the last thing the sisters need is a lot of discord. They are under enough stress."

Emma pointed at the package of stew meat on the counter. "Well, I'm going to cook up a big pot of stew, because one of the ways to relieve stress is to have a good, nourishing meal." She eyed Jennifer intently. "How much elixir did the sisters drink today?"

Jennifer sighed. "Too much, and that was my fault, but it was all they wanted. They claim it cures everything except terminal disease, and I'm sure they were hoping it would cure their broken hearts."

Tears filled Emma's eyes. "Well, my heart is broken, too. Just the thought of that sweet little animal . . ." She shook her head, and began cutting up the stew meat.

Jennifer gave her a hug. "I know, Emma. It breaks my heart, too. Ken was here earlier, and took a lot of pictures. John, Jr., is going to put the story in the morning paper, but I'm afraid all that is going to do is increase the sightings.''

''Meaning?''

''After the first radio report at noon, we were besieged with callers, all claiming to have seen Peaches. It's like everybody in town is frantically looking for Peaches, and I'm afraid it's only going to increase the confusion at this end. Zacharias was the one who suggested we keep the phone line clear, in case the kidnapper is trying to call. I called Ken, and he contacted the radio station so they could alert the public. We haven't had a call since. But with the story in the paper . . .''

At that moment, Frances wandered into the kitchen, with heavy footsteps. ''Got some chores to do outside,'' she said wearily. ''Fanny said she'd do 'em, but she's worse off than me.''

Jennifer kissed Frances's leathery cheek. ''Emma has everything under control here, so why don't I go with you?''

Frances nodded, and headed for the door.

Outside, the late-afternoon air was whisper soft, and Frances breathed in deeply.

"This is my favorite time of day. Well, I like the early-morning hours, too." Tears slipped down her cheeks. "Peaches likes mornings best. She likes to feed the chickens, and pull weeds in the garden. . . . I haven't said anything to Fanny, but I've been thinking. What if somebody took Peaches to sell to one of those experimental laboratories? Read about dogs and cats going to those places all the time. Know we don't have a place like that around here, but . . ."

Jennifer touched Frances's arm. "Don't, Frances. Don't torture yourself like that. You have to believe the culprit kidnapped Peaches, and that as soon as he makes his demands, he'll let her go."

They were standing in the garden now, and Frances shook her head. "Will you just look at all the vegetables that have to be picked? Didn't get to it yesterday, because we were too busy trying to make Peaches happy, and now another day is almost gone." She picked up a basket from the stack at the end of one of the rows, and began picking tomatoes. "You can pick green beans, if you have a mind to. You know, we'd give that man every cent we have in the bank to get Peaches back.''

Jennifer was about to tell Frances that there were a lot of folks in town who would be willing to offer financial help to meet the kidnapper's demands, when Wes yelled at them from the back porch. Fanny was on the phone with the kidnapper!

Chapter Six

Wes was on the phone with the sheriff, and Emma was trying to comfort Fanny, when Jennifer and Frances hurried into the kitchen.

Fanny was nearly hysterical, and Frances rushed to her sister's side. Wes held up a hand for silence, and spoke to the sheriff. "That's right, Jim. He just called. I answered the phone. He had a muffled voice. Male, I think. He asked for Frances or Fanny Cromwell, and sounded like he didn't much care which one he talked to. Frances was outside with Jennifer, so

Fanny took the call. I'd let her tell you what was said, but she's in pretty bad shape. . . . Uh-huh, I know. Well, here's the gist of it. The kidnapper isn't demanding money. He wants what he calls the 'formula' for the sisters' elixir. . . . Yeah, well that was my reaction, but if you'll think about it, it makes a lot of sense. The sisters only have X number of dollars in the bank. Once paid, that would be it. Can't get blood out of a turnip. But by getting the formula, there would be no end to the amount of bottles he could sell. He could go on the road and make a fortune advertising it as a cure-all for every medical problem known to mankind. . . . I know, he'd have to keep one step ahead of the law and the FDA, but if he's capable of kidnapping. . . . Uh-huh, and that's why it would sell. There are a lot of folks out there these days who are desperate for a miracle cure for what ails them. No doubt. That's why he was snooping around the house. When he couldn't find the recipe, he resorted to the kidnapping. The thing is, the recipe isn't written down. The sisters keep it in their heads. . . .

Yeah, that might be why he took those bottles of elixir, but without a chemist's analysis . . . Yeah, I know. His instructions were simple enough. First of all, no cops, or they'll never see the chimp again. They are supposed to write down the formula, put it in a sealed envelope, and take it out to the old cottage on Marshton Road. . . . That's right. The cottage where they were living before they bought the farm back from the bank. . . . Maybe, but I don't think we should try it. Something could go wrong, and—'' Wes took a deep breath. ''The cottage is empty now, and with no neighbors, it's a safe spot for the kidnapper to make the pickup. They are supposed to put the envelope in the mailbox. As soon as he has the formula, he'll call and tell them where they can find the chimp. We don't have a choice, Jim. We have to believe him. . . . That sounds good. We'll see you in about an hour.''

Wes hung up and sighed. ''The sheriff is on his way out. He doesn't like it, but he agrees we don't have a choice. We have to go along with it.''

Fanny swayed, and Wes reached out to steady her. "Let's go in the living room and wait for the sheriff," he said gently.

"Did the kidnapper give the sisters a time frame to deliver the recipe?" Jennifer asked, helping Frances into the living room.

Wes said, "Fanny?"

Fanny sat down on the couch, and shook her head. "Just said to put the envelope in the mailbox, and go home. Said it had to be Frances or me, or else."

Emma sat down on the edge of a chair, and pursed her lips in thought. "That sounds like he's going to be watching the cottage."

Wes said, "It also means he knows about the cottage, and the fact that Frances and Fanny were living there before they moved back to the farm."

Frances ran a hand through her wild, gray hair. "We lived in that little cottage for almost five years, and most folks in town knew about it."

Jennifer sighed. "Like everybody knew about the money you received from Elmer

Dodd, when and how you got Peaches, and about your famous elixir. Almost anybody could be suspect.''

''I don't mind giving that awful man the recipe if it brings little Peaches back safe and sound,'' Frances said raggedly.

Fanny nodded. ''Don't mind, either. Nothin' matters anymore but little Peaches's well-bein'.''

Wes took a deep breath. ''Then it's settled. We'll wait until the sheriff gets here before we make our plans. In the meantime, why don't one of you ladies write down the recipe.''

Frances nodded. ''We'll go upstairs and do it together. Fanny and me, well, we've got some talking to do anyway.''

After the sisters had gone upstairs, Emma let her breath out in one big swoosh. ''My, my, if that isn't the ticket. To think that somebody in Calico can be that evil. . . .''

''And greedy,'' Jennifer said.

Emma harrumphed. ''Well, I have to add the potatoes and carrots to the stew, but I have the feeling nobody is going to feel like eating tonight.''

After Emma left the room, Wes took Jennifer's hand. ''Want to go sit on the porch and wait for the sheriff? You look like you could use some fresh air.''

''I'd like that,'' she murmured, and followed him outside.

They sat in the porch swing, and Wes squeezed her hand. ''I don't know about you, but this wasn't what I expected. Peaches was kidnapped for the elixir? Boy oh boy. It makes me wonder how the culprit managed to come up with that scheme.''

''Or why,'' Jennifer said. ''Those ladies have been making moonshine for years; they've had the chimp for quite a while, so why did the culprit wait until now? I also have to wonder if Peaches knew the kidnapper, and that's why she went with him without putting up a fuss.''

Wes put his elbows on his knees, and rested his chin in his hands. ''Well, if that's the case, that sure counts out Zacharias Hardy and Charlie Biggs, because according to the sisters, Peaches doesn't like either one of them.''

Jennifer took a deep breath. A very deep breath. ''You actually think the kidnapper might be Zacharias or Charlie?''

Wes shrugged. ''It was a thought. Actually, Zacharias came to mind when we were talking about the intruder, and how the Cromwell men might have stashed some money in the house before they died. You have to go way back to understand my reasoning, sweetheart. Old man Cromwell died first, and Uncle Mitford about a year later. The sisters were in their forties at the time, bona fide old maids, and known all over town as 'the crazy Cromwell sisters.' Zacharias Hardy and his wife, Edith, were living on the farm across the road, and Zacharias was pretty good friends with Mitford, so even if he hadn't heard all the rumors about the Cromwell men being bootleggers, I'm sure he knew about it by way of association.''

''So you think, if the Cromwell men had stashed money somewhere in the house, Zacharias found out about it through Mitford?'' Jennifer shook her head. ''That's really reaching, Grandfather. For one thing, why would Mitford tell Zacharias, and not his own nieces? They couldn't have known about it, or they would have had plenty of money, and wouldn't have lost the farm to foreclosure. And then when you think about those long five years, after they lost the farm, when the house sat empty, well, it seems to me that Zacharias would have had every opportunity to look for the money.''

''I know, and that's why I dismissed that notion. And I've just about counted him out regarding the kidnapping, too. In order to profit from getting the sisters' recipe for the moonshine, he'd have to build a still so he could make it. Then he'd have to have a way of bottling the stuff, and getting out and about to sell it, because he sure couldn't sell it in Calico. That would mean a lot of traveling, and the old boy's truck can hardly make it across town, let alone across the state, or into some other state. It just seems like the kind of enterprise somebody like Zacharias wouldn't have the gumption or the know-how to take on.''

"Zacharias also told me that rotgut moonshine was what killed Mr. Cromwell and the uncle. He was upset at the time he told me, because the sisters were a little tipsy. It was clear he found the whole subject distasteful.''

Wes shrugged. ''Could have been an act, but I doubt it.''

"So what about Charlie Biggs?''

"He's new in town, so he's an unknown factor, sweetheart. But I have the feeling it didn't take him long to hear all about the 'moonshining' sisters, especially when they live right next door to the dairy. Maybe he's an opportunist, and saw this as a way of making some money. We all know Elmer Dodd pays his workers minimum wage, and . . .''

Jennifer shook her head vigorously. ''If you'd seen the concern in Charlie's eyes when he came to the back door earlier today, you wouldn't be thinking like that, Grandfather.''

"Well, I saw it when he helped me in

with the groceries, and when he was trying to comfort Frances, so I've counted him out, too."

"I'm glad, because I think he's a very nice man. And let's face it. Calico has grown a lot in the last few years, and there are a lot of people living here whom we know nothing about. Somebody could have been planning this from the time the sisters got the chimp."

"And that's reaching," Wes admonished.

"I know, but what other answer is there?"

Jennifer heard the car coming up the road, and sighed. "It's the sheriff. Let's hope and pray he can come up with some answers."

"Amen," Wes said, heading for the driveway.

Happy to see Ken Hering, too, Jennifer gave him a hug. "Hope you brought along your thinking cap as well as your camera."

Wes gave both men a brief rundown before they went in the house, but it was Ken who put it into perspective. "From everything you've said, I'd say the kidnapper is familiar with the elixir, and really believes it's a magic cure-all.''

''Meaning he's tested it first-hand?'' Jennifer asked.

''Yep, and I think the first place to start is to find out who the sisters have given it to, say in the last couple of months.''

The sheriff said, ''That's a good idea, but that won't solve our immediate dilemma, and that's letting the sisters take the recipe out to the cottage on Marshton Road. What's to say the kidnapper isn't a major bad guy, has no intentions of releasing Peaches, and plans on killing the sisters after they put the envelope in the mailbox?''

Jennifer shuddered. ''Grandfather and I thought we were reaching with all our theories and speculations, but you've topped us, Sheriff Cody.''

''But we can't count it out,'' the sheriff said, climbing the steps to the porch. ''But first things first. Right now, I want to talk to the sisters, specifically Fanny. Maybe she overlooked something regarding the phone conversation that might help us decide how to handle it.''

Frances and Fanny had returned to the living room, and for the first time since the kidnapping, they had smiles on their faces, and maybe even a shrewdness in their eyes, that was difficult to discern.

''We're mighty glad to see you, Sheriff Cody,'' Fanny said, patting the spot on the couch beside her. ''You sit a spell, and listen to what we have to say.''

The sheriff took off his olive-colored cap and sat down. ''I'd like to hear everything you have to say, Fanny, but would you mind if I ask you a few questions, first?''

''Don't mind,'' she replied.

Jennifer sat in a chair across from the couch, and exchanged glances with Ken, who remained standing with Wes. Emma was in the kitchen, but hurried out when she heard the sheriff's voice.

The sheriff smiled. ''We're all here, so we can get right to it.'' He opened a notebook, and pulled a pen from his shirt pocket. ''You said you didn't recognize the kidnapper's voice. Is that right, Fanny?''

"Didn't recognize it at all. Sounded like he had a handkerchief over the mouthpiece, or a bad cold."

"And he told you not to call the cops?"

"That's what he said. Said if we called the cops, we'd never see Peaches again."

"Did he specifically use the word 'cops'?"

"He did."

The sheriff scribbled something in the notebook, and frowned. "That's strange. Most folks around town refer to me as 'the sheriff.' Sounds like more of a city term to me, or he said it to throw us off the track. Did he say who he wanted to deliver the envelope?"

"Me or Frances, or both of us. Didn't matter none."

"But he didn't set a time frame?"

"Just said to put it in the mailbox in front of the cottage, and to go home. Said he'd call later, and tell us where to pick up Peaches."

"Did he say 'Peaches'? Or did he say 'the chimp'?"

"Said 'the chimp.'"

More scribbling, and then, "Can either of you recall who you've given a bottle of your elixir to in the last couple of months?"

Frances's brows drew together in thought. "Mr. Babkins wanted a bottle for his gout. Gave us a mighty fine-looking rooster in exchange."

Fanny nodded. "Gave a bottle to Annie, too. She wasn't a-sleepin' too good at night. She gave us a bouquet of flowers that time."

"Annie, who owns the florist shop?" the sheriff asked.

Frances nodded. "Let's see. Then there was Jasper Willis. Said he wanted it for his ailing wife. Didn't get nothing in exchange that time. Not that we expected it. That's not why we hand it out." She lowered her eyes. "Gave a bottle to Charlie Biggs, too. Oh, and a jar went to Pete Nelson. Said his back was bothering him."

The sheriff said, "Do you bottle the elixir in bottles and jars?"

Fanny replied, "We put it up in whatever we have."

Welcome to Athens-Clarke County Library!
You checked out the following items:

1. The chattering chimp caper
   Barcode: 33207003971845 Due:
   2007-05-17
2. The pink rabbit caper
   Barcode: 33207003872571 Due:
   2007-05-17
. Hell hath no curry a Pennsylvania
   Dutch mystery with recipes
   Barcode: 31040000625300 Due:
   2007-05-17

L-ATH 2007-05-03 17:32
u were helped by

''Why did you give a bottle to Charlie Biggs?''

''He's been under a lot of stress, workin' at the dairy. Said if he'd known what kind of a man Elmer Dodd was, he would've stayed in Omaha.''

Jennifer exchanged glances with her grandfather this time, and knew exactly what he was thinking. Charlie wasn't a likely suspect, but now there was no way they could count him out.

''Anybody else?'' the sheriff asked.

Fanny shook her head. ''Tried to give Zacharias a bottle when he was complainin' about his earache, but he wouldn't take it.''

The sheriff closed the notebook. ''One word of caution here, ladies. I don't want one word of any of this to get beyond the folks in this room.'' He smiled at Fanny. ''Okay, Fanny. What did you want to tell me?''

Frances grinned, and pulled a sealed envelope out of her pocket. ''This is the recipe. Didn't leave one single ingredient out, but Fanny thought we should add a few, so we did.''

"So the kidnapper won't have the real recipe?" Jennifer asked.

Fanny bobbed her head. "But that ain't the real reason. We added in a couple of 'secret' ingredients. Figure that nasty man won't waste no time makin' up a batch. Next, he'll taste it, and it won't be long after that, and he'll be a-wishin' he was dead."

"It won't kill him," Frances said. "It'll just make him mighty sick. So sick, we figure he'll be asking for help real quick."

The sheriff shook his head in amazement. "So sick, he'll get himself to a hospital because he'll think he's dying?"

Fanny nodded, and gave the sheriff an impish, toothy grin. "Might even have to call for an am-boo-lance."

Ken whistled through his teeth. "Sounds like those secret ingredients are pretty potent."

"Our daddy used to mix 'em up and use 'em on his horse when he'd get a sour belly," Fanny offered. "But they was good for human complaints, too, and only had one rule you had to follow. Couldn't mix 'em with elixir, else you'd get mighty sick.'' She grinned at Frances. ''Frances knows all about it, 'cause she tried it one time, and thought she was gonna die. Was sick a whole week.''

Frances paled at the thought. ''I was so sick, I wanted to die.''

Wes said, ''That's a brilliant idea, ladies, but I can't help but wonder—if he gets that sick, will he have the strength to get to a phone, or even have a mind to?''

''I can only go by what happened to me,'' Frances said. ''And I know I kept begging my daddy to call the doctor. He wouldn't. Said I wasn't dying, the sickness would run its course, and that I needed to suffer because I'd been a bad girl.''

Emma shuddered. ''Reminds me of the time I ate some skunk weed on a dare.''

The sheriff cleared his throat. ''We're dealing with a lot of ifs here. *If* he makes the elixir. *If* he drinks it. *If* he calls a doctor or goes to the hospital. But I believe we have to give it a try.''

Jennifer spoke up. "People go to the hospital all the time with digestive upsets, so how will we know if it's the kidnapper?"

Fanny tittered. "'Cause you get red, itchy blotches all over your body. Even after she was better, Frances itched for a month."

Ken chuckled. "Maybe the government should use that concoction as a secret weapon."

The sheriff said, "Uh-huh. Well, in that case, I'll alert Doc Chambers and the hospital. If somebody comes in with the tell-tale symptoms, I'll have enough probable cause to get a search warrant."

Jennifer added, "And if we find the still, we've got him."

"You betcha. Now we'd better make some plans for getting the envelope to the cottage on Marshton Road."

Frances waved a hand. "We got it all figured out while we were upstairs, Sheriff Cody. We decided one of us had better stay here in case that nasty man calls again. So we flipped a coin. I won. I'll be taking the recipe out to the cottage.''

''And I'll be going out there with you,'' the sheriff said. He held up a hand at the protests. ''It will be dark for one thing, and I'll make sure I'm scrunched down in the seat. If he's watching the cottage, he won't see me. This is just a form of protection, Frances.''

''He didn't say nothin' about hurtin' us,'' Fanny protested. ''Just said if we called the cops, we'd never see Peaches again.''

''And I want to believe that's what he meant,'' the sheriff said. ''But we're obviously dealing with a wacko here, and in my book, that means he's unpredictable.''

''I have a better idea,'' Ken said. ''I'll take Frances's place. We're about the same height, and if I wear her clothes and put a scarf on my head, nobody would be the wiser. That means if Mr. Wacko Unpredictable decides to pull something, we can both be ready for him.''

Tears filled Frances's eyes. ''You'd do that for us?''

"And a lot more," Ken said gently.

What followed would have been humorous, if it hadn't been for the seriousness of the situation. Ken settled on Frances's long black dress, and with a scarf over his red hair, he wouldn't have any trouble passing for Frances in the dark. Frances even gave him an old pair of granny glasses, minus the lenses, and he perched them on the end of his nose for effect. The whole thing brought smiles around, and smiles were what they all needed. That, and the heartfelt hope that the kidnapper was a man of his word, and Peaches would be returned safe and sound.

"Well now," Emma said, after Ken and the sheriff left. "I think we should use this time to eat. The stew is ready, and everybody needs a good nourishing meal."

"Don't think I could eat a bite," Fanny said wearily. "I keep thinkin' about little Peaches, and how alone she must feel. I keep wonderin' where she is. Is she warm? Does she have a place to sleep? She's used to a bed, you know."

Frances gave her sister a hug. "Little

Peaches is strong, sister. And she's tough. In no time at all, she'll be right here with us, getting into mischief. Now let's go eat. Emma went to a lot of trouble to fix that stew, and she's right. We need a nourishing meal.''

''Guess I could try a bite or two,'' Fanny said, giving Emma a wan smile. ''We want to thank you for all your help and generosity, Emma. And that goes for the rest of you. Don't know what we'd have done without our good friends.''

''Well, I'd say if your clever plan works, this nightmare is just about over,'' Wes said, trying to keep his voice cheerful. ''I don't mean we should celebrate yet, but it won't be long.''

Fanny brightened. ''And then we can have a party. A welcome-home party for little Peaches, with all our fine friends in attendance.''

Jennifer managed a smile, too, for the sisters' benefit, but it was hardly the way she felt. Ken and the sheriff could be walking into a trap, and if that happened, it would mean that Peaches was already . . .

Jennifer looked away quickly, so the sisters couldn't see the tears in her eyes.

"Are you cold?" Wes asked, putting an arm around Jennifer's shoulder.

They were sitting out on the front porch, waiting for the sheriff and Ken, who were now long overdue. "I'm okay," she said, resting her head against his hand. "Being out here is better than being in the house. I can't stand to see the sisters like that."

Wes sighed. "I know, but you can hardly blame them. I call it nervous energy."

"Uh-huh, well, Emma deserves a medal for going along with it, and offering to help."

"People handle stress in different ways, sweetheart, and it just so happens Fanny likes to clean house, and Frances likes to bake."

Jennifer listened to the hum of the vacuum cleaner, and shook her head. "Fanny is cleaning things that are already clean, and Frances is baking dozens of cookies. The last time I looked, Emma was polishing the furniture."

"Emma isn't polishing the furniture," Emma said, plodding out on the porch. "Emma just gave up. Those two have more energy than ten women put together."

"It's nervous energy," Wes said. "And the later it gets, the worse it's going to get. Me? I fidget. I don't want to mess things up, but I have this uncontrollable urge to call all the deputies, and tell them what's going on. I've gone over it a dozen times. It's a fifteen-minute drive to the cottage on Marshton Road. That's a half hour, all together. It wouldn't take much more than a minute to get the envelope in the mailbox, which means they should have gotten back a good hour ago."

Emma sat down in a wicker chair, and lowered her voice. "The sisters keep watching the clock, too, and the more time that passes, the harder they work. I know what they're thinking."

"It's what we've all been thinking," Jennifer said, feeling the chill of the night air, but welcoming it against her flushed cheeks. Thunderclouds were building up on the horizon, obscuring the sliver of moon.

''We're in for a summer storm,'' she said finally. ''And Peaches is afraid of thunder. . . .''

Emma let out a little cry. ''Look! Headlights!''

Not wanting to get the sisters' hopes up, they waited until the truck pulled into the driveway before alerting the sisters, and what followed was mass confusion, with everybody talking at once.

In the living room, finally, they listened to the sheriff's incredible account, leaving them all with the feeling that the kidnapper's game was far from over.

''Ken parked the truck with the headlights facing away from the mailbox,'' the sheriff explained. ''But when he opened the front of the mailbox, he found a note. Block letters, made with a marking pen. Said to take the formula to the telephone booth near the courthouse.''

Ken stepped out of Frances's dress. ''Found another note in the telephone booth. To make a long story short, we had to go to a good dozen places all over town, until we finally ended up in Calico Park, and left the formula under a rock in the rose garden. By that time, I was so upset, I wanted to stake out the park and catch the creep red-handed, until the sheriff reminded me that we had Peaches's life to consider. And that sure brought me around.''

The sheriff stretched, working the kinks out of his back. ''Now I'm convinced we're not only dealing with a wacko, but a demented one as well. I know, that probably means the same thing, but at this point in time, I don't feel like sorting it out. Nuts is nuts.''

''Well, thank goodness you're okay,'' Emma said tearfully. ''We were all mighty worried.''

''I had a few concerns, too,'' Ken said. ''There were too many places that were wide open, and the creep could have taken a potshot at me at any time. On a lesser note, I was worried about running out of gas.''

''So now we wait,'' Wes said, rubbing a weary hand over his eyes. He looked at

Emma. "Do you want to go home and try to get some sleep?"

Emma's reply was abrupt. "I want to be right here when that phone call comes in, Wesley Gray, and if I have to sleep standing up, I will."

The sheriff looked at his watch. "Well, I'm not leaving, either, but I'd better call Ida, before she sends for the National Guard."

"Well, nobody is gonna have to sleep standin' up," Fanny announced. "We got us lots of bedding, two beds upstairs, not countin' little Peaches's bed, and a nice couch down here that makes up in a bed. So, if anybody has a notion to take a nap, they can go right ahead."

The sheriff stretched again. "Do you have any of that stew left, Emma? Ken and me, well, we worked up quite an appetite."

Emma nodded. "Won't take a minute to heat it up, Sheriff."

"And we've got some peanut butter cookies fresh made for dessert," Frances offered.

Wes gave Jennifer a hug, and whispered

in her ear, ''Better have a cookie or two, sweetheart. It's going to be a long night.''

Long   and   nerve-racking,   Jennifer thought, wondering how long they were going to have to wait before the kidnapper called. But even worse was wondering if he would call at all.

Chapter Seven

It was almost 7:00 A.M. when Jennifer found Frances in the kitchen, baking biscuits. They had all managed a nap at some point during the night, but nobody had actually gone to bed, nor had anyone slept well. At the moment, the men were playing cards at the dining-room table, discussing the comprehensive story in the morning paper, that now was truly yesterday's news, and Emma was outside with Fanny, helping her with the chores.

"I thought you came out here to make

coffee,'' Jennifer said, giving Frances a hug.

"I made coffee," Frances returned. "I also decided our good friends should have one of our special breakfasts. This is a new day, little Jennifer, and I think we should begin it with renewed hopes and smiles. I'll admit along about three o'clock A.M., when that nasty man hadn't called, I felt like having a screaming fit. But then I decided all that would do was upset everybody, especially Fanny, and wouldn't accomplish a thing. We've got us some clouds covering the sun this morning, but I'm not going to let them cover my heart. Peaches will be coming home today. I know it; I can feel it."

Praying Frances was right, Jennifer said, "Is there anything I can do to help?"

"With breakfast? Well, you can find Fanny and tell her I need two dozen eggs. We didn't gather them yesterday, so there should be plenty. Oh, and tell her to get the big ham out of the smokehouse. I have to put it on to simmer early, so it will be ready to bake by this afternoon."

"If you're going to bake the ham for us . . ."

Frances adjusted her glasses on the bridge of her nose, leaving a smudge of flour. "The ham is for our celebration dinner, Little Jennifer. I told you when Peaches gets home, we're going to have a party."

Wishing she had Frances's optimism, Jennifer hurried out to find Fanny.

Jennifer looked up at the sky, and felt like smiling for the first time in hours. Yes, the clouds were covering the sun, but oh, how glorious the sky looked, wearing shades of peach, cream, and gold. The air was whisper-soft, too, giving no hint of the storm that was building up to the south.

Jennifer found Fanny and Emma in the garden. Emma was working on a row of corn, while Fanny picked cucumbers.

"Well, good mornin', little Jennifer Gray," Fanny said, giving Jennifer a wide smile. "When we left the house, you was a-snoozing in a chair."

"Good morning," Jennifer returned. "Why didn't you wake me up?"

"No need for that. Nobody got much sleep last night, so even a snooze or two is important."

Emma poked her head around the row of corn, and smiled. "Good morning, honey. You know, your granddaddy grows some mighty fine corn, but *this* corn beats all. Each ear must be over a foot long." She walked over and placed the basket on the ground near Jennifer. "Just look at that. I only picked a dozen ears, and the basket is full."

Fanny beamed. "And it's tender and sweet enough to eat right out of the garden without cookin'. But we've got us a secret way of doin' it to keep those ears tender, even after cookin'."

Wondering if the sisters had some "secret" fertilizer, too, Jennifer relayed Frances's message. "Oh, and she wants you to get the large ham out of the smokehouse."

Fanny's blue eyes danced. "That's 'cause we're gonna have a celebration party tonight for Peaches's safe return."

Emma said, "Ummm, well maybe you'd

better wait a day or two, Fanny...."
Emma caught the expression on Jennifer's
face, and cleared her throat. "Well, I guess
Peaches wouldn't mind having a party right
off."

Fanny stood up and wiped her hands on
her apron. "Got to get the eggs for
Frances."

"I can do that," Jennifer said.

Fanny shook her head. "I'd better do it.
We got us a couple of mean chickens, and
we have to handle 'em in a special way.
But you can get the ham out of the
smokehouse."

Jennifer waved a hand toward a small
building between a stand of peachleaf willow trees and the barn. "Over there,
right?"

"That's right. Our daddy built that
smokehouse when we was just little tykes,
and we've never had to do a thing to it,
'cept repair a few boards on the roof. The
big ham is hangin' to the right of the door.
Don't need to cut it down. The rope has
got a loop over a big nail. If you need a
light, the switch is to the right of the door,

too, and you can use the little step stool if you have to. Me and Frances don't need it, 'cause we're so tall, but you might.''

Jennifer made her way across the dusty barnyard, where chickens pecked at every pebble and twig and scratched up little dust storms in their eagerness to find a morsel of food. Jennifer had to smile, and told one old red hen, "If you would stay in the chicken yard where you belong, you'd have plenty of food!''

The Rhode Island Red looked up at her with beady eyes, made low, clucking sounds in her throat, and went back to pecking at the ground.

The door to the smokehouse was closed, and the minute Jennifer opened it, she was met with the wonderful aroma of smoked meats. Some of the things that were hanging from the rough, knotted beams defied description, and she quickly bypassed them and headed for the hams. There were four of them, with the largest weighing at least fifteen pounds.

Not letting herself think about what was going to happen if Peaches didn't come home today, or if the kidnapper didn't call, Jennifer turned on the light and looked around for the step stool. When she couldn't find it anywhere, she was about to go and ask Fanny if it might be somewhere else, when she caught sight of the stool behind a long butcher-block table on the other side of the room. Deciding the only way to reach it was to walk around the far end of the table, Jennifer was headed in that direction when a flash of metal on the floor caught her eye. She picked up the object, turned it over in her hand, and felt every terrible thing that happens to a person when they've received a sudden jolt to their senses. Rubbery knees. Racing heart. That horrid, sick feeling when you can't seem to catch your breath. She was holding the tailpiece of a syringe, or dart, used in a Cap-Chur gun, also called a "flying hypo," used to administer medicine to wild animals, but also used to administer tranquilizers. At that moment, she knew how the kidnapper had gotten Peaches out of her bedroom without causing a ruckus. He'd shot her with a tranquilizer dart, waited until it had taken effect, and simply carried her out through the window.

Feeling confused and sick, but still keeping the sisters' best interests in mind, Jennifer decided on using a subtle approach to this, at least until she could talk to the sheriff. And so she put the tailpiece in a pocket, set about to getting down the oversize ham, and then casually carried it back to the house.

Fanny and Emma were in the kitchen, having a heated debate with Frances. Frances claimed brown eggs tasted better than white, Fanny said white eggs tasted the best, while Emma claimed they all tasted the same to her. An egg was an egg was an egg.

Jennifer placed the ham on the table, washed her hands, and managed a smile. "You'd better go easy on breakfast if you expect us to eat all that ham for supper, Frances."

Frances grinned. "No matter what I fix for breakfast, you'll be hungry again by suppertime. We're having corn on the cob, too, and Fanny's special recipe for oven-roasted potatoes.''

''And I'm makin' my special peach cobbler,'' Fanny announced. '' 'Course, I gotta go get some peaches off the tree before I do that. Or else I gotta use a jar or two we put up last year.''

''Sounds wonderful,'' Jennifer said. ''Are the guys still playing cards in the dining room?''

Frances shook her head. ''They're out on the front porch, drinking coffee. Pour yourself a cup, little Jennifer.''

Jennifer poured coffee into a mug from the large blue-and-white speckled pot, tried to keep her hands from shaking, and said, ''If you don't need me in here, I think I'll join them.''

''You go right ahead,'' Fanny said. ''We got us enough cooks in the kitchen.''

Emma had been eyeing Jennifer intently, and said, ''I can take the hint.''

Frances clucked her tongue. ''Fanny didn't mean anything by that, Emma. And right about now, we can use your help. You promised to show us how you make that quick peach jam that's ready in one hour, but everybody thinks you've been cooking it all day.''

Jennifer escaped while she could, and hurried through the house.

''Well, here she is!'' Wes said with a smile. Did you get the right ham?''

''I did,'' Jennifer said, sitting down in a wicker chair. She placed the coffee mug on the small table beside the chair, and reached into her pocket. ''I also found this.''

The sheriff took the object, and frowned. ''It looks like the tip of some kind of a dart.''

Jennifer took a deep breath. ''It is, though technically it's called a syringe. It's the tailpiece of a syringe used in a Cap-Chur gun, Sheriff Cody. It's also called a 'flying hypo.' Simply put, the darts are used to either administer medicine or capture wild or unruly animals. If it's a capture, tranquilizers are used. I believe that's how the kidnapper got Peaches out of her bedroom.''

''Whoa,'' Ken said.

Wes said, "Boy oh boy."

"I know. That's the way I felt. I couldn't believe what I was seeing at first. I haven't said anything to Emma or the sisters, because if I'm right, and that is how Peaches was abducted, some really bad things could be involved. For one thing, there are five principles when you use a Cap-Chur gun, and if the person doesn't know what he's doing . . ."

"Boy oh boy," Wes repeated. "I don't like the sounds of that."

The sheriff nodded his head in agreement. "And the five principles?"

"Number one, the safety factor. It's imperative the user of the gun knows the weight of the animal, or has a very close estimation within the critical safety margin. If not, the drug used could prove fatal. Number two, using an appropriate level of physical and psychological immobility and tranquility. In other words, if an inappropriate amount of the drug is given, the animal could die by way of injury or stress. Number three would be the rapid onset of the drug. The longer the time it takes for the drug to take effect, the more the animal is open to injury, so you can see, the safety factor runs a fine line. Number four, if too much of the drug is given, recovery can be difficult at best. Number five is the recovery time after being injected. Longer is not better. And, did the person use an antidote to bring Peaches around quickly? Or is there an antidote for the tranquilizer used? Some don't have any, and an animal can die as a result.''

The sheriff grimaced, and opened a notebook. ''Okay, let's go back. You found this in the smokehouse?''

Jennifer nodded. ''When I went to get the ham. Fanny said I might have to use the step stool, and when I went to get it, I saw the tailpiece lying on the floor close to the back of the room.''

''Did you see anything else?''

''No, but then I was so shook up, I didn't look. I think it's obvious the kidnapper used the smokehouse as a place to hide until it was time to make his move, and while he was there, he inadvertently dropped the tailpiece. He wouldn't want to put on the light to look for it, or maybe he didn't know he dropped it. The darts come in sections, and maybe he had several.''

''Is it actually called a tailpiece?'' the sheriff asked.

''Yes, it is, and there are several other sections that make up the complete dart. Do you want me to describe what it looks like?''

He handed her the notebook. ''Uh-huh, and while you're at it, maybe you could draw a sketch? Might help us later, if we happen across other sections.''

Jennifer sketched the tailpiece first. ''This is the tailpiece, or the rear end, and it's the section you're holding in your hand. The fuzzy tip acts like the feathers on an arrow, allowing the dart to fly in a straight line. That metal piece attached to the other end of the tailpiece is called an O-ring seal. Next is the Cap-Chur charger containing a light explosive substance, which is set off when the dart hits the animal. Next is the rubbery material, almost like a cork, that acts as the plunger. Next is the syringe barrel, which holds the drug, another O-ring seal, and finally the nose plug, containing the hypodermic needle.''

''And you shoot the darts from a regular gun?'' the sheriff asked.

''No, the darts are shot into the animal using CO_2, just like a pellet gun.''

''Rifle?''

''Yes, for long range, like eighty yards or so. Otherwise it's a pistol-type. I'd say this was a pistol-type, because of the short distance from the window to the bed. If you're wondering about the brightly colored tailpiece, that's so that the particular section can be found more easily in the field after the dart has been shot into the animal.''

''Does the gun make a noise when it's shot?'' Wes asked.

''It's about as loud as a pellet gun.''

Ken said, ''That's not very loud. What about availability, say for the average Joe Citizen?''

''There are several manufacturers in the U.S., but we deal with one manufacturer in particular, because we believe they make the best product.''

"Then you have a Cap-Chur gun at the clinic?" the sheriff asked.

"We have two of them. One pistol, and one rifle." She smiled slightly. "You never know when we're going to encounter a raging bull, or a nasty dog. Seriously, we've only used the rifle once on a combative horse, and we've never had to use the pistol."

"So, are they easy to get?"

"Well, I don't suppose the general public would know how to go about it, but yes. All you have to do is place an order and send along the payment."

"What about the drugs?"

"Not so easy, unless you're a vet, or have a bona fide reason. Just like certain veterinarian medicines can't be purchased by the general public." Jennifer looked at her watch. "Ben should be at the clinic now, and I think we'd better start from ground zero here. I'm going to give him a quick call, and make sure our guns are where they are supposed to be, but I don't want to call from the kitchen."

"Let's use the radio in my car," the

sheriff said. "Nettie can patch you through to the clinic."

The call only took a couple of minutes, and by the time Jennifer and the sheriff returned to the front porch, all that had been established was the fact that both Cap-Chur guns at the clinic were accounted for, giving them a dozen different avenues to explore, and leaving them more confused than ever.

Wes finally said, "What about the dairy? Wouldn't they have a gun like that?"

Ken said, "More important, what about Collin Dodd? He's the resident vet, and would know all about using a Cap-Chur gun."

Jennifer nodded. "It's very possible the dairy has a Cap-Chur gun or two, but then so would the Keya Paha Game Refuge, and it's only twenty miles away. But as far as Collin Dodd being the kidnapper, I think that's *really* reaching, Ken. He lives at the dairy, so there is no way he could build a still on the QT."

"Unless he built it somewhere else."

The sheriff said, "What if Elmer is in on

it with him? He's still disgruntled over having to give the sisters all that money. What if this is his form of revenge? Collin would also have the time and the money, with Elmer's backing, to travel all over selling the elixir. Collin was in the barber shop just the other day telling everybody that he couldn't wait until he could get enough money together so he can hit the road. And he made a big to-do about how much he hates Calico.''

''He's been saying that from the first day he arrived in Calico,'' Wes reasoned. ''That doesn't make him a kidnapper.''

Ken said to the sheriff, ''Did you call the boys in Lincoln after the sisters received the call?''

The sheriff chuckled without humor. ''And tell them what? That the kidnapper wants the formula for the sisters' elixir? Next they'd ask me what was in the sisters' elixir, and if I couldn't tell them, Calico would be swarming with ATF agents before you could blink twice.''

Jennifer frowned. ''The sisters aren't selling the elixir, and they certainly haven't hurt anybody. As a matter of fact, they've probably done a lot of good, though I suppose it's mind over matter. You know— you give two people who have the same complaint a pill. One is given a placebo without knowing about it, and he feels better immediately.''

The sheriff sighed. ''I've been sworn to uphold the law, but I'll have to admit I've turned my head when it comes to those ladies and their moonshine, because I never once thought they were making illegal hooch, which I believe breaks down to alcoholic content. Old Tom Brown makes his own beer, and the Pollsons make a fine blackberry wine, and it's all perfectly legal. But now I think I'd better check into it further, for their sakes as well as my own. I'm not saying I think the Feds are gonna come swooping into town wearing riot gear if they get wind of this, but I sure don't want any unexpected surprises.''

Wes shook his head. ''And you think the sisters are going to give you the recipe?''

''They might, if I tell them what's at

stake. If not, I'll take a bottle to the hospital lab for analysis.''

"Take what to the hospital for analysis?'' Emma asked, stepping out on the porch.

"Where are the sisters?'' the sheriff asked.

"Chin-deep in breakfast. They wanted me to tell you all it won't be long. Frances is frying the sausage now.''

The sheriff lowered his voice, explained what he planned to do, and added, ''I have their best interests at heart, Emma. And because we don't know what's ahead—''

"I understand all that,'' Emma broke in. "But what I don't understand is the look on Jennifer's face, and it's the same look I saw when she brought the ham into the kitchen.''

The sheriff handed Emma the tailpiece. "I'd better let Jennifer explain.''

"That's the tail end of a dart used in a Cap-Chur gun, Emma. I found it in the smokehouse when I went to get the ham, and I think the kidnapper used a tranquilizer dart to get Peaches out of her bedroom.''

Emma puffed out her cheeks. ''Well, if that just don't beat all. So, who would have access to one of those kinds of guns?'' Her eyes narrowed. ''Collin Dodd. He's the dairy vet.''

''He's on the list, but the Keya Paha Game Refuge isn't far from here, either, and now that I think about it, any number of ranchers in the area might have the same kind of gun, for any number of reasons. My real concern is not knowing who was at the other end of that gun, Emma, because if the person didn't know what he was doing, well, I don't want to even think about the outcome. That's why I didn't tell you about it when I was in the kitchen. The less the sisters know, the better.''

''Oh, dear, and they are so up. They believe with all their hearts Peaches is coming home today.''

The sheriff looked at his watch. ''And the day is fading fast. After breakfast, I'm gonna have a look around the smokehouse, and then I'm gonna have a little talk with the sisters. If they won't give me the recipe, I'll take a bottle to the hospital. Ken, I'd like to make use of your investigative reporter skills. Make a list of all the ranchers around that might have a Cap-Chur gun, and go talk to them. Wes and Emma, I think you should stay here with the sisters in case the kidnapper calls. If that happens, call Nettie. As my dispatcher, she can relay the message to me, no matter where I am.'' He looked at Jennifer and grinned. ''Guess you know what I want *you* to do.''

''Go to the dairy and poke around?''

''I don't want anybody to know about the dart's tailpiece, or what we suspect, but you can still ask a lot of questions. I'd also be curious to know if Elmer and Collin are at the dairy. Oh, and if you get the chance, I'd also like you to talk to Charlie Biggs. I'm sorry to say, he's still on my list. He lives and works at the diary, and if they do have a Cap-Chur gun, he could've swiped it to use that night.''

Ken shook his head. ''It doesn't seem likely he'd build a still in his cottage, Sheriff, so do you have any thoughts on that?''

"I don't have any thoughts that amount to a hill of beans on anything, Ken. And until the sisters receive that call..." He shook his head. "*If* they receive the call. Maybe we'd better go in the house and see if we can hurry things along, because the sooner we can get started on this, the better."

Emma muttered, "Well, best you all remember this. We might not feel like eating, but the sisters have gone through a lot of trouble to fix us a special breakfast, so each and every one of us had better make a vigorous attempt."

Ken chuckled. "Or else we all might be the recipients of flying pots and pans."

The sisters had the breakfast buffet set out on the dining-room table, and what a feast it was! Poached eggs with honey-bread toast, fluffy biscuits and rich cream gravy, sausages browned to perfection, and a huge bowl of fruit, generously laced with elixir. Even those with the most sluggish of appetites dished up generous servings, and the conversation was friendly and upbeat while they enjoyed every bite.

And then out of the blue, the sheriff said to the sisters, "You think of everybody in this room as your friends, right?"

The sisters bobbed their heads.

"And you trust us?"

"You wouldn't be here if we didn't trust you," Frances said.

The sheriff cleared his throat. "Well, keeping that in mind, I think it's time we had a little talk. I was going to talk to you about this alone, but I've decided it might be better if we are all a part of it, because everybody in this room cares a great deal about you, and what happens to Peaches." This time, the sheriff took a deep breath. "It's come to my attention that the FBI in Lincoln might find some interest in your elixir. I already alerted them to the kidnapping, but that was when we thought the jerk was after money. Now, if they find out he's after the recipe for your elixir—and there are a number of ways they could find out— they might wonder what's in the elixir that would make it important enough for the kidnapper to abduct a family pet, and in such a dramatic fashion. You following me so far?''

Fanny pursed her lips. ''You're sayin' that because our daddy and uncle were moonshinin' men, they might think we're doin' the same thing?''

''Something like that. What happened to Peaches is terrible, but I surely wouldn't want to compound it by having the two of you in trouble with the ATF.''

''The AT who?'' Frances asked.

''The Bureau of Alcohol, Tobacco and Firearms. That falls under the Department of the Treasury, but . . .''

Fanny let out a whoop of laughter. ''You hear that, sister? We might have the Feds a-beatin' down our door.''

Frances didn't share her sister's amusement, and scowled. ''If you're asking us if we've got something in our recipe that might get us into trouble with the Federal government, the answer is no.''

''Can you swear to that?'' the sheriff asked.

Frances marched over to the sideboard

and picked up a dog-eared Bible. "We might not get to church much, but that don't mean we ain't believers. This Bible was our mama's, rest her soul, and she used to read it to us all the time." Frances held the Bible out with one hand, and placed the other hand on top. "I swear, on the memory of our mama, Daddy, and Uncle Mitford, there isn't one thing in our elixir that can get us or anybody in trouble. I'll admit our daddy and uncle were moonshining men, and when they died, the recipe was handed down to us. But we never much liked that recipe, and so we changed it. Took us a while to get it right, but we did, and now it's just what it is—a remedy for all kinds of ailments. The only alcohol in it is a good dollop of berry and apple wine. . . . You want me to give you the recipe?"

Fanny added, "Ain't got no poison in it, if that's what you're worried about."

The sheriff smiled. "I didn't think it did, and no, I don't want the recipe. I just wanted your word."

Frances snorted. "Well, you've got it. I know you're all concerned about our well-being, but best we remember that little Peaches is the one we need to be worrying about. Fanny and me, well, we've done just about all we can do to keep our spirits up, but now it's going into another day. . . .''

Wes said, ''We know that, Frances, and the sheriff has some plans hopefully to speed things along.''

Fanny made a face. ''If that nasty man would just make up a batch and taste it, it could be over in a shake.''

Frances shook her head. ''Don't want that to happen until he calls, and tells us where Peaches is.''

The sheriff said, ''Well, we've made some plans, ladies. Emma and Wes are gonna stay with you for a few hours, while we—''

The ringing phone cut him off, and everybody froze.

The sheriff waved a hand at Jennifer. ''You take it. Maybe you'll recognize his voice.''

When everybody was in the kitchen, Jennifer picked up the receiver, and said, ''Hello?''

"Who is this?" a deep voice asked.

"Jennifer Gray. Who is this?"

"Dr. Ward from Calico General Hospital. The sheriff told Dr. Chambers and us to call this number if somebody showed up with certain symptoms."

Jennifer could hear her heart pounding in her ears, and said to the others, "It's the hospital." To Dr. Ward, she said, "Severe abdominal discomfort and big, red itchy blotches all over his body?"

"That's it. He came in about an hour ago, and thought he was dying. I would have called you then, but the blotches didn't pop out until just a few minutes ago, and quite frankly, I've never seen anything like it as long as I've been a doctor, and that's a good long time."

"And you're not likely to again," Jennifer managed to choke out. "Did he give you a name?"

"John Smith, but I have the feeling that's the same as John Doe."

"Did you ask to see some identification?"

"Yeah, but he said he was in such a

hurry to get to the hospital, he left it at home.''

''Can you describe him?''

''Uh-huh. Tall, thin, with black slicked-back hair. Dark beady eyes. He was wearing jeans, a plaid shirt, and manure-caked boots. He looks familiar, but I can't place the face.''

Jennifer said, ''Did he say anything about the chimp?''

''No, he didn't, but then, he was in pretty bad shape. Still is. We're admitting him, just like the sheriff asked us to, but we would have anyway. One question. The sheriff didn't say anything about swelling extremities, among other things.''

''And his extremities are swollen?''

''Swelling up as we speak. When I left him, his legs and arms were getting puffy, and his belly looked like the Pillsbury Doughboy's.''

''The sheriff is here, Doctor, so maybe you'd better talk to him.'' Jennifer handed the receiver to the sheriff, dropped to a chair, and said to her captive audience, ''The doctor just described Collin Dodd.''

Chapter Eight

Bedlam followed the phone call from the doctor, while everybody talked at once. It wasn't a surprise it was Collin Dodd, but now that they knew, dealing with it was much more difficult than expected. And there were still so many unanswered questions.

Finally, the sheriff yelled for silence. "I know, it isn't a surprise, yet it's still a shock. But more important right now is how we're gonna handle it. If he'd called first, to let us know Peaches's whereabouts, I'd arrest him right now. But he didn't, and that puts the whole situation into a different perspective.''

"Not necessarily,'' Wes said. "At the moment, Collin Dodd doesn't know why he's ill. And for sure, he's in no condition to run. I say we confront him. He's a weak man, and I'm not just talking about his ailment. Maybe if he knows we're on to him, he'll confess.''

"And if he doesn't?'' Emma reasoned. "He has all the symptoms Frances and Fanny described, but how will that hold up in a court of law? It seems to me the only way you can prove he's the kidnapper is to find Peaches, and the still, and something else that links it all to him.''

Jennifer said, "Which brings up another question.''

Ken muttered, "I can think of more than one.''

"I know, but we have to handle one question at a time.'' She looked at Frances and Fanny. "I know you make the elixir in an old bathtub, because I remember seeing it in the barn out on Marshton Road. So, does that mean it can be mixed up in a sink or a bathtub inside of a house?''

Fanny said, ''Yes and no. It can be mixed up anywhere, but it's gotta be cooked. We've got us a big cast-iron pot. We put all the ingredients in the pot, and put it over an open fire pit in the ground. We make up one batch at a time.''

''That's right,'' Frances said. ''And after it's cooked, we put each batch in the bathtub.''

''When the bathtub is full,'' Fanny added, ''we let it sit for five or six days. Then it's ready to put in jars or bottles.''

''What happens if you don't let it sit?'' the sheriff asked.

''Nothin','' Fanny said. ''But it don't taste as good.''

The sheriff shook his head. ''Then you don't use a regular still.''

''No, we don't,'' Frances replied. ''Our daddy and uncle did, but we don't need to. Not the way we make it.''

''So, you could just as easily cook it on the stove inside the house?''

Fanny wrinkled her nose. ''We could,

but we don't, 'cause it stinks when it's a-cookin'. Besides, the big cast-iron pot wouldn't fit on our stove.''

''Did you write any of that down when you gave the recipe to the kidnapper?''

''Nope.''

''So the kidnapper doesn't know the elixir is supposed to be cooked?''

Fanny's grin was sly. ''Nope, and if it ain't cooked, it tastes like somebody's dirty socks at the end of a cattle roundup.''

''Uh-huh, so along with writing down some 'secret' ingredients that didn't belong in the recipe, you didn't write down any instructions?''

Frances nodded. ''Now we got us the culprit in the hospital, so it looks like we did the right thing.''

''Uh-huh, well, what I'm getting at here is, without the instructions, do you think Collin might have made it in his bathtub, inside his . . . Never mind. He lives in a trailer, and trailers don't have bathtubs.''

Wes scratched his head. ''Maybe he made it in the kitchen sink or, for that matter, in a pot on the stove. I think you'd better take a look at his trailer, Jim.''

"I plan on it. I'm also going to talk to Elmer, and see what he has to say. I still haven't counted out the fact he might be a part of it. I'll go do that now, and then we can all go to the hospital, and confront that repulsive man."

"I ain't goin' nowhere," Fanny muttered. "Maybe he turned Peaches loose, and she's on her way home."

Frances put an arm around Fanny's shoulder. "As much as I'd like to give that man a piece of my mind, I'll stay with Fanny."

"And I'll stay, too," Emma said.

The sheriff nodded. "Give me a half hour to talk to Elmer, and—"

Wes raised a hand. "I don't like the idea of wasting that much time, Jim. While you talk to Elmer, we'll go to the hospital. We're dealing with unknown variables here, and there is no way to predict how long Collin is going to be ill. Let's get to him while he's down."

The sheriff nodded again. "Then I'll

meet you at the hospital when I've finished questioning Elmer. Might even bring him along, depending on his answers.''

Wes said, ''Jennifer, Ken?''

''We're ready,'' Jennifer said. ''As far as I'm concerned, we can't get there soon enough.''

There was no way to describe Collin Dodd's condition, other than to say he looked as bad as he felt. He was in a private room, and the shades were drawn, but it was still easy to see his swollen extremities, and the ugly red splotches all over his face, neck, and arms. The nurse had put up the guardrails because he kept thrashing around, and it was more than apparent he wasn't in the mood for company.

''Can't imagine what you're doing here,'' he mumbled, squinting at Jennifer.

Jennifer put up the shade, and smiled. ''I'm not alone, Collin. Ken Hering and my grandfather are here with me.''

The sun was poking through the clouds now, and Collin raised a hand as though to ward off the rays filtering into the room.

"It's too bright. My eyes hurt. You say your grandfather is here? Oh, no! I'm dying, and he's here to give me my last rites!"

Ken stepped up to the bed. "And I suppose you think I'm here to write up your obituary? No such luck, Collin. You're going to live, and pay the piper for your sins."

Collin whimpered feebly, "I don't know what you're talking about."

Jennifer said, "You will soon enough. First of all, we're interested in what made you so ill."

Collin groaned. "That's it. I've got some terrible disease. Am I contagious? Is it gonna affect the whole town? I don't like Calico much, but I wouldn't wish this on anybody."

"You're not contagious," Jennifer said. "Now, can you tell us what made you so ill?"

"Well, if I don't have a disease, it had to be the drink. See, I was playing cards with Charlie Biggs one minute, and the next minute—"

Jennifer broke in. ''Charlie Biggs? Was that in your trailer or at his cottage?''

''His cottage. We both had the day off, and we were killing some time. We were listening to the radio, too, for updates on the chimp, and then Charlie put out some nuts and crackers, and mixed us a drink. I know, it was pretty early in the day to be drinking, and I would've settled for coffee, but Charlie was insistent.''

''Do you know what was in the drink?'' Wes asked.

''Don't know, but Charlie said I'd like it. He mixed two drinks, set them on the table, and then he got a call from Elmer.

He'd left the water running in the main yard again, like he always does, and Elmer wanted him to take care of it.''

''And did he?'' Ken asked.

''Yeah, and by the time he got back, I was as sick as a skunk, and wanted to die. Charlie drove me to the hospital, and the whole way, he kept saying I'd better tell the hospital I was John Smith or Joe Green, because if I didn't, he was gonna be in a whole lot of trouble.''

Jennifer felt her heart accelerate. ''Did he say why?''

''Nope, but I figured it was because he'd mixed the drinks, and felt responsible.''

''Did Charlie say he thought it was the drink?''

''In a roundabout way, though he didn't explain. I didn't have my billfold on me, so when the attendants got me out of the car and into emergency, I told them I was John Smith. And I've been too sick to say much else since.''

''Does Elmer know you're in the hospital?'' Wes asked.

''Nope, and when he finds out . . . I can just hear him telling me that that's what I get for taking up with Charlie Biggs. See, my uncle doesn't think too much of Charlie Biggs. Says he's lazy and worthless, but then he accuses me of being lazy and worthless, too. Well, maybe I am, and that's why Charlie and me . . . well, that's why we get along.''

''Then you think it was the drink that made you ill?'' Wes asked.

''Asked and answered, Pastor. It had to

be the drink. Three swallows, and I was a goner.''

Jennifer pulled some change out of her pocket, and said, ''I'm going to use the pay phone in the corridor to make a call.''

Wes nodded. ''Go with her, Ken. I'll stay with Collin.''

Out in the corridor, Jennifer took a deep, ragged breath. ''I know what you're thinking, Ken. You'd much rather it be Collin Dodd than Charlie Biggs, but can you come up with another explanation?''

''Unfortunately, I can't, and I don't think Collin is lying.''

''Nor do I, and that's why I'm calling the dairy. Maybe I can catch the sheriff before he leaves.''

Jennifer looked up the number for the dairy in the phone book, and made the call. Elmer answered on the first ring, and she wasted no time getting to it. ''This is Jennifer Gray, Mr. Dodd. Is the sheriff still there?''

Muffled voices, and then, ''This is the sheriff, Jennifer.''

Jennifer's words tumbled out. ''Collin

was playing cards with Charlie Biggs in his
cottage when this happened, Sheriff Cody.
Charlie made a couple of drinks, and then
got called away by Elmer, because he'd left
the water running. . . ."

"I know."

". . . and Collin was sick after only a
few . . . You know?"

"Charlie Biggs is here with us, Jennifer.
He feels terrible, and blames himself for
Collin's condition."

"Well, isn't he responsible?"

"Well, maybe in a roundabout way, but
he had no idea what 'special' ingredients
were in the elixir when he made those
drinks."

"Wasn't that the idea?"

"Yes, but you're putting the blame on
the wrong man. Charlie was out of the
elixir Frances had given him earlier in the
week, so he used a bottle he got from
Zacharias."

Jennifer sucked in her breath. "He got a
bottle from Zacharias?"

"He did. He was in the company store
this morning, when Zacharias moseyed in,

carrying a brown paper bag. He wanted to know if the store carried blackstrap molasses, because he'd run out.''

''Let me guess. One of the 'special' ingredients in the elixir?''

''Yep, one of twelve secret ingredients. I just talked to Frances, and she confirmed it. Charlie told Zacharias the store didn't carry it, but he had some in his cottage, because he was a glutton for homemade gingersnap cookies, and bakes a batch whenever he can. Zacharias went to the cottage with Charlie, and while he was there, he pulled a bottle out of the bag. He said he'd found a recipe for homemade wine in one of his wife's old cookbooks, and wanted Charlie to give it a try. Said he couldn't do it himself, because he has an ulcer. Charlie said he would, and would let him know if it was any good, and that was the end of it, until Collin showed up to play cards.''

''Uh-huh, and Charlie mixed the drinks.''

Jennifer said, ''But before Charlie could take a taste himself, Elmer called him away, and when he got back to the cottage, Collin had already fallen ill?''

''That's about it. Charlie says Zacharias came back to the cottage shortly after he returned from the hospital, but hurried off after Charlie told him about Collin, and all but accused him of giving him a bottle of liquid poison, even if it was his wife's special recipe for wine.

''I wasted no time getting over to Zacharias's house, but he wasn't there. I checked the property, but didn't find the still, or anything remotely suggesting he'd made a batch of elixir. Can't go into the house without a search warrant, and that's what I'm working on now. I've got a call in to Judge Stoker. I also have a deputy watching Zacharias's house.''

''Is his truck gone?''

''It is, and I have all my deputies looking for it.''

''We're on our way, Sheriff. There's nothing more we can do here.''

''There's nothing more I can do here, either,'' the sheriff said. ''So I'll meet you at the Cromwell house.''

Jennifer hung up, trying to suck air into her lungs. "I'll tell you what that was all about on our way to the sisters' house, Ken. Come on. Let's get Grandfather!"

It took fifteen minutes to get back to the house, and by that time, Wes and Ken had been filled in.

The sheriff was waiting for them in the driveway, and his mouth was little more than a grim line. "Deputy Aliva spotted the truck on Route 5, heading out of town. He's bringing Zacharias in now. I'll meet them at the jail, but first . . ." The sheriff shuffled from one foot to the other. "Zacharias told the deputy that Peaches is in his cellar. He admitted to using a 'dart gun' on her. If you can believe it, he borrowed it from Wilber Hyde, claiming he had an ailing cow. Well, everybody knows Zacharias got rid of his cows years ago, so that just proves old Wilber is so tied up with that cattle ranch of his, he doesn't know what's going on beyond the tip of his nose."

Jennifer reached for the medical bag in the back of the Jeep, and felt tears close to the surface. "That also tells me we had an amateur at the shooting end of that gun, and heaven only knows what kind of condition Peaches is in. We can't wait for the search warrant, Sheriff Cody."

"I know. I already called Judge Stoker, and he gave us his blessing."

"Have you told Emma or the sisters?"

"No, and I don't think we should, until . . ."

Wes sighed. "Well, if we all disappear across the road, they are going to wonder, so I'll go in the house and make up some excuse as to what you're doing."

Ken said, "Maybe you should try to prepare them, in the event . . ."

Jennifer shook her head. "No, Ken. We have to believe Peaches is okay. We just have to!"

Ken hung his camera around his neck and muttered, "Well, I'm not taking any pictures unless we find her alive."

Jennifer shivered, and headed across the road.

*   *   *

Remembering the mess Zacharias left behind in the sisters' kitchen, it was no surprise to see the house in total disarray. Dust covered everything, their shoes stuck to the kitchen floor, and every dish and pot and pan was dirty.

Like the Cromwell house, the door to the cellar was off the kitchen, and it was closed. Jennifer wasted no time opening the door and flipping on the light switch, and knew immediately by the stench of rotted food and sickness that Peaches was in a bad way. Praying they weren't too late, she hurried down the stairs, peering into the dimly lit, cluttered cellar.

The sheriff and Ken followed, and both men were cursing under their breaths.

Not able to see the chimp right off, Jennifer called out, "Peaches, it's Jennifer. . . ."

Ken said, "Maybe he's got her stuffed in a box."

Jennifer raised a hand. "Listen . . ."

The low, chortling sounds, typical of a chimp, were clear now, but so very, very weak. Jennifer managed to choke out, "This way. She's over in the corner!"

Jennifer made her way around a stack of boxes, and gasped in horror. Peaches was under a workbench, still wearing her yellow pajamas, and her little ankles had been tied together with a white nylon cord. There was a cord tied around her waist and the table leg, too, giving her approximately two feet to maneuver.

"Oh, sweetie!" Jennifer cried, using a surgical knife to cut the cord. "Oh, you poor little thing!"

Weakly, Peaches wrapped her long arms around Jennifer's neck, and buried her face against her chest.

After a quick examination to make sure the chimp was stable enough to be transported, Jennifer fought back a waterfall of tears, and said, "I have to get her to the clinic immediately, but I don't want the sisters to see her like this. . . ."

Ken said, "I'll go tell the sisters— Whoa, what should I tell them?"

"Just that we found her, I'm taking her to the clinic for a checkup, and that they can come to the clinic if they want. Oh, and tell them she'll need clean clothes, and it wouldn't hurt to bring along her favorite toy.'' Peaches was making soft, sobbing sounds in her throat now, that twisted Jennifer's heart. ''It would help if you'd get my Jeep, too, Ken, and pull it around to the back door.''

''Will do,'' Ken said, heading for the stairs.

The sheriff wiped his brow with a handkerchief. ''Looks like Zacharias threw her food at her, the way everything is splattered around.''

Jennifer noted the moldy bread crust, rotted potato skins, and hunks of wilted lettuce, and grimaced. ''He's been feeding her garbage, Sheriff, and I don't see a trace of water anywhere. That's why she's showing all the classic signs of dehydration. I have to call Ben, so he can get things ready. . . .''

The sheriff picked up Jennifer's medical bag, and followed her up the stairs. ''I'll call Ben,'' he said. ''And then I'm going to look around. Even with Zacharias's confession, I'd like to find the proof he made the elixir. Wouldn't hurt if I could find the dart gun, either. I'm going to throw the book at him, Jennifer, and I'm going to enjoy every minute of it.''

Ben was waiting for Jennifer in the rear parking lot of the clinic, and his rugged face was lined with concern. Peaches was curled up in a fetal position on the seat beside her, and when Ben opened the door, concern turned to anger. ''I hope Zacharias Hardy does heavy time for this, Jennifer.'' He carefully picked Peaches up in his arms, and held her close. ''Come on, little lady. Let's get you inside.'' To Jennifer, he said, ''I've got the IV ready to go, and everything out for the tests I figured you'd want to run.''

Jennifer returned, ''At the moment, I anticipate doing a blood workup, and because she's dehydrated, it's imperative to find out if her kidneys are functioning. She's filthy, but the cleanup will have to be last, and heaven help us if the sisters see her before we get to that point.''

"Where are the sisters?" Ben asked. "I was sure they'd either be with you, or right behind you."

Jennifer placed Peaches on the emergency room examining table and said, "Ken and my grandfather are trying to detain them, though I don't imagine they'll be too far behind. Will you try to comfort them when they get here, and assure them that Peaches is going to be just fine?"

"Is she going to be just fine?" Ben asked, looking down Peaches's throat with a flashlight.

"Her blood pressure is a little erratic, but other than that, her vital signs are normal enough, so I'd say the prognosis is good. But I hate to think what would have happened if we hadn't found her when we did. Another day or two . . ." Jennifer broke off. "Let's start the IV, get a blood sample, and go from there."

It was four o'clock that afternoon when Jennifer walked out into the waiting room with Peaches in her arms, where the sisters, Emma, Wes, Ken, Elmer Dodd, and

Charlie Biggs had been patiently waiting. Peaches was wearing a clean pink pinafore, smelled of baby powder, and finally pulled her lips back against her teeth in a broad smile. She was still under a good deal of stress, and weak, but she belonged at home, where the sisters could give her all their love and infinite care.

Although there wasn't a dry eye in the room, everyone was silent as the sisters stood up with outstretched arms. And Peaches lifted her arms to them. And then everybody was weeping and talking at once, as the sisters gathered their dear little friend close, murmuring words of affection.

Jennifer cleared her throat, and smiled through her tears. ''Peaches won't be up to par for a few days, but she's going to be just fine.''

Peaches was in Fanny's arms now, and Fanny gave the chimp a giant hug, before saying, ''We don't know how to thank you for savin' Peaches's life, little Jennifer Gray. You and that nice Ben Copeland.'' Tears rolled down her leathery cheeks. ''I thought that man was my friend, and that just shows you how dumb an old lady can get.''

Frances clucked her tongue. ''Best we forget about everything that happened before this very minute, sister, and start looking forward to tomorrow. But I do have one thing to say.'' She turned around and looked at Elmer Dodd. ''I'm sorry your nephew got that fake elixir instead of the real culprit, Elmer, but maybe you'll feel a mite better knowing he won't be sick long. A couple of days, maybe less. As I understand it, he didn't drink much of the concoction.''

Elmer cast his eyes downward. ''Nobody could've predicted how all that was gonna turn out. And it wasn't your fault. You were trying to find out who kidnapped Peaches, and I'd say your plan was foolproof.'' He shuffled from foot to foot, and said awkwardly, ''I want you to know you can have all the tubs of cottage cheese you need for Peaches. Lots of protein. Good for her.''

Frances smiled. ''Well, we don't give her cottage cheese all that often, Elmer, because her little system don't handle dairy products that good, but now and again, if she has a hankering for some, we'll take you up on your offer.''

Fanny spoke up. ''We want to thank you all for bein' here with us, and just as soon as Peaches feels up to it, we're havin' a little celebration party. Now, I think we best get little Peaches home, and tuck her into bed.'' She heaved a big sigh. ''It's gonna be mighty lonely now, with everybody a-goin' home, but we'll have our good memories.'' She grinned at Ken, who was holding his camera. ''Though I suppose we could wait a couple of minutes while Ken Hering takes some pictures.''

While Ken took a series of pictures, Wes pulled Jennifer aside and asked, ''Have you talked to the sheriff?''

Jennifer nodded. ''He called about an hour ago. Zacharias is in jail. We didn't get into too many particulars, because I didn't have the time, but I'm going to stop by the sheriff's office on my way home.''

''Did he find the Cap-Chur gun, or anything else that might be incriminating at Zacharias's house?''

''He found the gun, several syringes, the drug, the formula, and a tub in the bathroom full of the phony elixir, along with numerous empty jars and bottles.''

''The deputy spotted him heading out of town, so I don't understand. Was he planning to leave all that incriminating evidence behind?''

''I think he panicked, Grandfather. He told the sheriff that after he gave Charlie that bottle of what he *thought* was the genuine stuff, he wondered if he'd done the right thing, and got nervous. He knew Charlie had tried the sisters' elixir, so I can only assume he was wondering if Charlie was going to recognize it, and make the connection. Don't forget, he told Charlie it was his late wife's recipe for wine. Anyway, he went back to see Charlie, and that's when he found out Collin had gotten ill after consuming a portion of his drink. I think that's when he panicked. He left with a half tank of gas, some pocket change, and the clothes on his back.''

"Doesn't sound like he would have gotten very far, even if the deputy hadn't spotted him."

"No, it doesn't. Would you look at Peaches? She's posing for the camera."

Wes said, "Speaking of Peaches and the sisters, do you think somebody should spend one more night with them? Emma brought it up earlier, and said she wouldn't mind it at all. In fact, I think she really wants to be a part of Peaches's homecoming."

Jennifer smiled. "I think it's a wonderful idea, Grandfather, but then right about now, the whole world is wonderful. At least our little world in Calico, Nebraska."

Wes kissed Jennifer's cheek. "Well, seeing's how Emma is going home with the sisters, and will no doubt feast on succulent baked ham tonight, how about if we have a little celebration of our own? I'll pick some fresh veggies from the garden, barbecue a couple of steaks, and then we can spend the evening over a mind-boggling game of Scrabble."

"It sounds wonderful, Grandfather. It

seems like I've been away from home for a year.''

''Then it's a date,'' he said, giving her a hug.

Jennifer gave Wes a hug in return. ''I love you,'' she said softly.

''And I love you, sweetheart. More than you'll ever know.''

It was after five when Jennifer walked into the sheriff's office, and although he looked exhausted, the smile on his face was wide. ''I take it the sisters have taken Peaches home?''

Jennifer sat down in a chair across from his desk, and nodded. ''And it was quite a reunion. They'll be having a party soon, and you and Ida are invited. Nettie, too. I take it she's gone home?''

''She has, but she'll be coming back in a little while with Zacharias's evening meal. A party, huh? Sounds like fun.''

Jennifer waved a hand toward the hallway that led to the block of jail cells. ''I have no desire to see that man, but I sure would like to know what kind of an excuse he gave you for behaving in such a disgusting fashion.''

''He didn't give me an excuse, Jennifer. He told the truth. He got the idea one day when he overheard Charlie tell Frances that if they ever decided to sell their elixir, they'd probably make a fortune. If you want my opinion, I think he has a screw loose in his head, but that will be up to the courts to decide.''

''Was he planning on bottling the elixir and selling it?''

''I think that was his original plan, but he obviously wasn't thinking it through.''

''Did he show any remorse for what he did to Peaches?''

''Nope, and I had to sit on my hands the whole time I was questioning him. Nettie took his statement, and she broke three pencils in the process. You could almost see steam coming out of her ears.''

''Well, by the condition Peaches was in, I'd say she was the last thing on his mind. He told me the other day that he thought the chimp's disappearance was probably the best thing that had happened to the sisters, other than getting the old homestead back from 'crooked' Elmer Dodd, and that if they insist on having an animal around, they'd be better off with a cow, dog, or cat. Something that could earn its keep.'' Jennifer took a deep breath. ''He also kept Peaches drugged, Sheriff. He'd shoot a hypodermic into her hide a couple of times a day. We found that out when we did the blood workup. Fortunately, the doses were low. I think his only concern was keeping her quiet.''

The sheriff scowled. ''Yeah, well, now he has something else to be concerned about. Saving his own rotten hide.

''How is Fanny taking it? I mean, he was her boyfriend, for lack of a better word.''

''She's upset, but she'll get over it. I think if nothing else, this whole trying ordeal has taught the sisters what's really important to them, and family is at the top of the list. And Peaches is a part of their family.''

The sheriff sighed. ''Poor little critter. I'm glad she's going to be okay.''

Jennifer stood up. ''Believe me, we all

are, Sheriff. Now, I have to go home. Grandfather is going to barbecue steaks, and then we're going to spend the evening playing Scrabble.''

''That sounds normal.''

''It's very normal, and it sounds wonderful.''

Outside, Jennifer raised her face to the warmth of the sun and the gentle breeze coming in off the river, and waved at familiar faces as she made her way to Fenten's Ice Cream Parlor. Wes hadn't said anything about dessert, and so she planned to surprise him with a quart of chocolate fudge ripple. It was indeed a night to celebrate, and give thanks for Peaches's homecoming, and for being alive.